THE SMALL BUSINESS
MILLIONAIRE

Also by Steve Chandler & Sam Beckford:

9 Lies That Are Holding Your Business Back

Also by Steve Chandler:

RelationShift (with Michael Bassoff)

100 Ways to Motivate Yourself

Reinventing Yourself

50 Ways to Create Great Relationships

100 Ways to Motivate Others (with Scott Richardson)

The Joy of Selling

17 Lies That Are Holding You Back

Ten Commitments to Your Success

Two Guys Read Moby Dick (with Terrence Hill)

The Story of You

THE SMALL BUSINESS MILLIONAIRE

Steve Chandler & Sam Beckford

A Novel of Heartbreak and Prosperity

Robert D. Reed Publishers • Bandon, OR

Robert D. Reed Publishers
P.O. Box 1992
Bandon, OR 97411
Phone: 541-347-9882 • Fax: -9883
E-mail: 4bobreed@msn.com
web site: www.rdrpublishers.com

Typesetter: **Barbara Kruger**
Cover Designer: **Grant Prescott**

ISBN 1-931741-73-5, 73-6

Library of Congress Control Number 2006900410

Manufactured, typeset and printed in the United States of America

To Kathy and Val

Chapter 1

The oppressive humidity and haze of a southern Michigan summer caused Jonathan to roll up his windows and turn his car's air conditioner on as he drove the last miles down Woodward Avenue before pulling into Royal Oak and his favorite restaurant, The Sunshine Inn.

Life was good for the young millionaire, but not so good that it couldn't be made better by ordering a fine and simple meal in a setting that gave him peace and comfort.

His old red Ferrari, rumbling below the floorboards as it always did, was like a caged animal he never let out to play. But it still felt powerful to him after all these years of multiple repairs and tune-ups. Jonathan had bought the used classic car five years ago because it was a dead ringer for the 308 GTS featured on his favorite TV show, *Magnum, P.I.*

Jonathan wasn't always comfortable admitting that Magnum had changed his life. But there was something in Tom Selleck's lighthearted ways that always got the job done and made the bad guys wish they hadn't crossed him.

As life went on, Jonathan would continue watching cable reruns of *Magnum*, but he had a harder time admiring his hero. For one thing, his hero was nearly always broke! And for Jonathan, that condition got old very fast, and so he decided to add his own skill to the character, the skill of knowing how to generate wealth, no matter what the job was.

Jonathan pulled his red beauty into the parking lot of a charming made-over strip mall, the kind that Royal Oak was so proud of after having reinvented itself from being a boring suburb of Detroit to an attractive arts and restaurant community.

Putting his laptop and books under his arm, he push-kicked the door to the Ferrari closed and walked into the restaurant. Jonathan looked around for a while before seating himself at a quiet table by the window and waited until a large, overweight gentleman who looked to be anywhere between 50 and 70 came to the table with a menu and a pitcher of water.

"Good afternoon, fine sir," said the older man with a slight accent that suggested the old country somewhere, although Jonathan couldn't place where.

"Hello, Frank," said Jonathan. "Today I'll start with some iced tea. It's hot and muggy out there."

Jonathan had often described the Sunshine Inn as having a typical American menu, with many exceptions. Because Frank was not typical. From food-proud Polish and Italian stock, he was a masterful cook, and people often came from miles away to visit Royal Oak's best-kept secret restaurant. Jonathan often wondered why this great restaurant was such a secret, but he also enjoyed being able to get a table any time he wanted.

And he was always amused and inspired by watching Frank, who had not missed a day at work even when his wife died unexpectedly last winter while helping him put up Christmas lights on their house.

Frank said, "There's no special today, sir. Just what's there in front of you on the menu."

"Well, you know that's always fine with me," said Jonathan. "You've got the best food in town, Frank. But you seem a little preoccupied. Is everything okay with you?"

"Oh, me? Sure," said Frank, rather unconvincingly.

After the death of his wife, Frank and his daughter Jennifer just kept carrying on the work at the restaurant, and Jonathan was touched. Frank had told him that Jennifer, who looked to Jonathan like a younger, blonder version of Sandra Bullock, was attending business school at Wayne State in Detroit. Frank confessed in a weak moment that he had named his daughter "Jennifer" after Jennifer Warnes, the original lead singer in the musical *Hair*, which was Frank's all-time favorite album. Frank not only took his daughter's name from the musical, but also the name of his restaurant after the hit song, "Let the Sunshine In." And as if that weren't enough of a tribute, his own name Frank Mills was also the name of a song sung by Warnes on the cast album. The minute Frank heard that song he knew he would no longer be Frank Milciewski. If Royal Oak could reinvent itself, so could Frank. Shortly after changing his name, he quit his job on the General Motors assembly line and opened his restaurant.

Today, as usual lately, the restaurant was nearly empty. And the couple at the table in the far corner had already paid their bill and were settling some small disagreement over coffee, which Jennifer was refreshing every five minutes or so.

Jonathan ordered the grilled steak salad, a specialty at the Sunshine Inn, and watched Frank as he wrote the order down, then erased it and wrote it again.

"Frank," said Jonathan to get his attention.

"Oh, yes, sir," said Frank as if snapping out of a dream.

"Please sit down a minute. I'm not in a hurry."

Jonathan always enjoyed the fact that Frank was an out-front, hands-on kind of owner, and whenever Jonathan came in to dine he would ask Frank what was new on the menu. Frank was always experimenting with a "special" in the kitchen. But today the air of experimentation was gone, and the mood seemed gloomy.

Frank pulled out a chair and sat across from Jonathan. Jonathan moved the yellow tulips in the center of the table over to the side so that they could see each other and then pushed back a little in his chair and slouched in an inviting way, shrugging his shoulders in a "what's up?" kind of way.

"Well, yes, I'm a little nervous," said Frank. "I am waiting for some news."

Jonathan softened into a relaxed, warm expression, and a slight smile passed over his face, as if slightly amused that a man Frank's age could be as uptight as a schoolboy waiting to see the assistant principal. He wondered what kind of situation would prompt that, but guessed it had something to do with money.

Frank said, "We're waiting to see if our loan will be approved. Our loan for the restaurant. You've probably noticed that we haven't been exactly packed full lately, and if this loan doesn't come through for us, I don't know if I can keep this going any longer, as much as I love it, and as much as it has meant to my family over the years."

On earlier visits, Frank had told Jonathan about what the restaurant meant to him. How he had worked in the automotive plant for 20 years on the assembly line, saving every penny he could for his dream of running a family restaurant.

Jonathan listened a little longer to Frank talk about how the loan would be a final bandage to cover the wound of a slow summer, and thought deeply and quickly inside himself about whether to say something that Frank would not want to hear. Finally, he decided to go for it. Sometimes the truth is the greatest kindness of all.

"Frank, for my own sake, I hope your loan is *not* approved, because I really like this restaurant," Jonathan said quietly and carefully, not wanting Frank to miss a word.

Frank said nothing. He looked at Jonathan for a moment as if he had completely misunderstood, although he knew he hadn't.

"Sir, did you just say to me that you hope it's *not* approved?"

"That's what I just said to you, Frank, because that's what I do hope."

Frank started to speak, stopped to smooth the tablecloth, and then started again.

"Sir, that doesn't make sense to me," said Frank. "If you like it so much here, why wouldn't you want us to stay open?"

"I do want you to stay open."

"You do? Then please explain."

"I don't want you to just stay open, as in 'just barely' stay open. Because I want to enjoy coming here with the old happy Frank serving me, not some depressed person. It's hard to enjoy a meal served to you by a depressed person or a worried person. It's a matter of me wanting the whole experience, Frank. What's your restaurant called? Sunshine? I want the sunshine as well as the great cooking."

"But, sir, we need the money."

"I understand that you do need something. You need something to change, so that you are successful and happy doing this. But the loan is not the answer. In fact, the loan will be bad for your business, not good."

"How can money be bad for a business?" Frank laughed bitterly. "Money is what a business lives on. It takes money to make money. Everybody knows that. Everybody says that."

"Not always, Frank, and not this kind of money," Jonathan said. "You have to pay this kind of money back! And not only that, this kind of unearned money might put you to sleep. It will definitely postpone your breakthrough. It could do great harm. That's why I hope the loan is denied!"

Frank poured himself some water and then watched as the chunks of lime in the pitcher settled to the bottom. He grabbed the handle of the pitcher and turned it sharply so the lime slices started floating back up. Frank shook his head slowly.

"With all due respect, sir," Frank said, "I don't think you know what you are saying. You are a music teacher, are you not? What do you know about running a business?"

"I know enough."

"And, besides, what is this thing…this 'breakthrough' you talk about? Do you know something about this restaurant that I don't?"

Jonathan smiled at Frank and offered his hand across the table. Frank looked puzzled but shook Jonathan's hand. Jonathan pulled his chair closer to the table.

"I have an appointment in an hour,." Jonathan started to say. Frank jumped up, looking embarrassed, as if he didn't understand anything about this whole conversation.

Frank said, "Oh, I am sorry!"

"No, don't be sorry, just bring me my salad and let me work on my notes for my appointment, and we will continue this conversation when I'm here next. I'll be back in a week, and I'll have a clear mind, and I can answer all your questions. I want you to succeed, Frank."

"Of course, sir," said Frank. "But I hope you don't mind if I disregard what you said today, because I…we…really are praying for that loan to come through."

"I understand," said Jonathan. "I've been in your same position, and believe me, I understand. I've done some loan-praying myself."

Frank made an awkward bow and retreated to the kitchen to help prepare Jonathan's order.

⁂   ⁂   ⁂

Later that night, as Frank was cleaning up, he looked over at his daughter Jennifer who was sitting at the far corner table going through the day's receipts and entering figures into her accountant's journal.

"That young man you like so much...." Frank said to Jennifer who did not look up. "What is his name? The music teacher who looks like Harry Belafonte...when Harry was young...I saw him at the Fisher Theater...." Frank was groping to express himself.

"Dad...." Jennifer said as she looked up, annoyed. "First of all, I don't admire him in the way you think, and I don't know who Harry Belladonna is or whoever it is you're talking about."

"Belafonte!" Frank said. He began singing, "Day-oh! Day-oh, daylight come and I wanna go home...."

"Whatever," says Jennifer, rolling her eyes. "I'm sure our gentleman customer would appreciate that. I'm sure he would feel honored by that stereotype."

Frank stopped and looked at the broom he was holding. Soon he was sweeping again, but still staring at Jennifer.

"Strange," he said.

"What's strange?"

"He said he hoped our loan wouldn't get approved."

"You told him about the loan?"

"Well, you know he's always so nice. He's always so interested, he almost feels like more of a friend than a customer...."

"Okay, and he said what? That he hoped the loan would *not* get approved? Why was that?"

"Something about a breakthrough. We can't have our breakthrough if we get the loan."

Jennifer looked back down at the accounting journal she was filling in. She gave a huge sigh.

"Breakthrough," she said. "Maybe he wants us to break on through into bankruptcy? Close the business? Why doesn't he just eat somewhere else? He could have his own little breakthrough that way."

"Jennifer, he means well!"

"Well, he was right about one thing," she said. "We need something."

"We need the loan!" said Frank. "If we get the money, we can get all caught up with our creditors, and hope for a good fall season. Football weather, people coming in to get a bite to eat before the big game...."

Frank's voice trailed off as if he knew that this was just another version of his yearly fantasy. The thought that something great was always coming and that the outside circumstances in his life would start to break his way. He had always heard that if you work hard enough, things will come your way. He had always believed it. After all, it was just common sense, wasn't it? The harder you work, the more likely you were to succeed. Yet somehow this common sense wasn't paying off for the restaurant. It seemed like the harder he worked the deeper in debt he got.

Jennifer was gathering her paperwork together for the night, looking over at her father and hoping to say the right thing. She had never worried this much about her father. It used to be that her father was always the one to make the family happy. Even when her mother died, it was her father, the one who had lost the most, who kept the family in good spirits and gave them the strength they needed to carry on. But now it was different. There was something about this situation that was different.

"It's different now," said Jennifer. "There's something about these debts we have that are different. I have a feeling about this, Daddy, and I don't like this feeling I have...I don't think there's a way out, and if that music teacher is saying that he hopes we don't get the loan so we can end our misery sooner, then maybe I agree with him...."

"No, that wasn't what he meant," said Frank. "Somehow he thought there might be some breakthrough or something good that wouldn't happen if we got the loan...I don't know...look at us! We are so desperate we are listening to a music teacher, trying to find hope anywhere! What can a music teacher know?"

"He dresses well," said Jennifer, her face losing its worry and starting to get wistful. "And I like his car. He doesn't look like a starving artist to me, and he's always got these books and that laptop and that hand-held computer thingy, so it's not like he's some homeless...."

Frank began to laugh.

"Oh, so you don't like him in that way...."

Jennifer began to laugh, too, "Stop it! Let's go home! I'll lock up. Tomorrow is a new day, Mr. Frank Mills. Perhaps some sun will shine tomorrow on the Sunshine Inn."

"It's in the bank's hands," said Frank.

Chapter 2

Frank was waiting in the bank's lobby for what seemed like forever when the young woman called out, "Mr. Mills!"

"Yes," said Frank standing up and putting the *People* magazine back on the table. He had just been reading about some of Donald Trump's bankrupt projects and properties and wondering how Mr. Trump kept getting loans when it was so hard for Frank, who had never been bankrupt once.

Frank followed the young woman into an office where he was greeted by a thin college-boy type who was dressed like he was ready for a funeral. The boy shook Frank's hand a little too hard and gestured toward the chair in front of his desk.

"Sit down, Mr. Mills," the young man said. "I'm Blair Downing and I'm your loan consultant here at First Mutual and I just want to thank you for banking at First Mutual and hey, I keep meaning to come by and sample your restaurant, what is it...Italian, right?"

"No, sir...."

"Well, whatever, but I'm afraid I have some bad news for you, Mr. Wells, because...."

"Mills."

"Right, Mills. I apologize. I see so many people. But we will not be able to give you this...to fulfill your request at this time...because we just couldn't make the numbers tumble for you here...."

"Tumble?"

"Yeah, I'm sorry. I went to bat myself on this one, but we just couldn't get it crunched for you...just missed...because of the mortgage, and you'll see in the memo, we just don't see any trends here to give us any sign of an upturn ahead."

"What about football?"

"Excuse me?"

"When football comes, people come in...."

"Mr. Mills, you don't understand. This is a business and this is a business decision. It sounds like you want it to be kind of old school...old school trust. But money is tight now and we don't have enough to go on...."

Frank didn't hear the rest. Blair Downing was droning on but it just sounded like noise to him, like some Peanuts cartoon on TV he used to see Jennifer watch when she was a little girl...a distant muted horn honking out of the mouth of some boy who lived all day with numbers but never once came in for one of Frank's specials. Frank got up in the middle of the muted horn noise coming out of Blair Downing's mouth and excused himself. The boy offered Frank the loan papers across the desk and Frank waved them off.

"Save them," Frank said. "And don't throw them out."

"Don't throw them out?"

"We will have a breakthrough, and I will come see you. I will bring you a meal."

"A meal? Well, that would be nice...."

"So I can watch you eat it. Watch you thank me and apologize."

Before the youth could reply, Frank was out the door and into the late afternoon's clouded sunlight looking for his truck in the bank parking lot and wondering whether he even wanted to return to the restaurant. Ever.

Frank climbed into the driver's seat, put the key in the ignition, and just sat there. He didn't know what to do or think next. For some reason, he wanted to see the music teacher. Not that he thought it made any sense to put any hopeful thoughts into some music teacher he barely knew, but something inside him was telling him to seek him out.

Frank had never been to the House of Harmony where Jonathan said he worked, but once he had recommended that his sister send his niece Katya there for music lessons and everyone had been happy. It was out at the end of Pinetree, past the city limits, if he remembered right, so Frank just drove in that direction, only half-caring whether he even found the place. Finally, there it was, almost hidden among huge birch and maple trees that cast shadows across the building. Frank parked his truck in front of the sidewalk leading up to the entrance. He got out and walked into the building.

"Is Mr. Jonathan in today?" Frank asked at the receptionist's desk as the sound of a violin came from the back rooms and the pounding of little feet ricocheted into his ears from down the corridor.

The woman smiled at Frank and shook her head, "We don't have a Mr. Jonathan here, is there somebody else who can help you?"

"No Jonathan? He is the owner."

"Oh! Mr. Berkley! Jonathan Berkley? Yes he is the owner, but I'm sorry, he hasn't had an office here for years. His office is in Detroit. Do you want me to help you make an appointment with that office?"

"I thought he was a music teacher."

"Oh, he is. Or, he was. But that was long ago. He runs all our studios now. Should I call him for you?"

"Oh, no...I'll see him soon...he comes by my business a couple times a week."

Frank started to smile and offer a small bow to the woman.

"I'm so sorry you came to the wrong location," she said.

"No, I did not," said Frank. "No, I did not. You have a beautiful studio here. Someday I may come learn to play music here myself."

"We have an excellent senior program."

"Senior?" Frank said. "Of course, senior program. May I ask you, do you know the music to *Hair*? The Broadway musical?"

The woman laughed, "That was a little before my time, sir. But I am sure we could find any music you like."

Frank was humming some of the music to *Hair* as he waved and turned for the door. Almost as an afterthought he turned back and called to the receptionist from the doorway.

"I am Frank Mills!" he said, as if it meant something.

The receptionist smiled. She watched with intrigue as Frank walked away, wondering if she had done enough to help him.

Chapter 3

A week later, Jonathan was sitting in the far corner of the restaurant late at night, the same corner Jennifer did her books in after closing. He was finishing his dessert and sipping a cup of decaf coffee when Frank appeared at his table with a slight bow.

"Well, sir, you got your wish," said Frank.

"What do you mean?" said Jonathan.

"The loan," said Frank. "The loan was not approved and now we are in real trouble, and if I am not being too much trouble, I would like to know why you thought this bad, bad thing would be so good."

Jonathan closed his laptop and set it on the chair next to him.

"Sit down, Frank," said Jonathan as he cleared some room on the table. "Why don't you tell me why this situation—the refusal—not getting the loan—is such a bad thing. To begin with. What were you going to use the money for, if I may ask?"

"Because look around you!" said Frank. "Don't you see, sir, we don't have enough customers! I need to advertise to bring in customers and I have too many bills at the radio station and the newspaper already. I can't run any more ads until I get them caught up, and the loan was going to do that."

"Advertising is expensive, isn't it?" said Jonathan.

"Yes!" said Frank. "Because you can't advertise just once, you have to repeat. What is it that she said? You have to build your name IQ."

"Name I.D?" said Jonathan.

"Name I.D. and brand and all of that," said Frank. "You have to build and repeat, and that's what's so expensive."

"So who is she?" Jonathan asked. "Who is she that tells you that?"

"My consultant," said Frank. "Rhiannon. From the newspaper. She is very nice, although she talks faster than any man can follow…but she is trying so hard to help us…."

"She is a sales person, Frank," said Jonathan. "Just remember that. She is here to sell you. If you don't believe she is selling you, look at all the bills you have paid—and unpaid—to her. So let's start right there. Her goal is to sell you ads. Your goal is to have lots of people come into the restaurant. They are not always the same goal."

"She is trying so hard to help me!" Frank nearly yelled, "She is lying to me? She is deceiving me?"

"Well, no, probably not," said Jonathan. "She herself probably doesn't know what works and what doesn't. But she is definitely not helping you. Look around you. As you say."

Frank poured himself a glass of water.

"She is helping me," Frank said softly.

"If there are no customers coming in from the ads, she is not helping you," said Jonathan, just as softly.

Frank looked skeptical. His ad rep from the paper, Rhiannon, was so nice, calling him "Mr. Mills" and bringing her family in to eat every so often. Frank trusted her completely. How could she just be "selling" him? It always made sense what she told him. You have to get your name out there. You have to let people see the name Sunshine Inn over and over before it will sink in.

Jonathan gestured to the waiter, a young African American who came to the table in a hurry.

"More coffee?" the waiter asked.

"Please," said Jonathan, "And remember it's decaf, I have to sleep tonight."

"You must go home and sleep," said Frank.

"Not yet, Frank," said Jonathan. "Not until we straighten this one thing out. I won't sleep at all until we get something straight about bringing customers into your restaurant, okay? Let's start right here. You want to bring customers in, true? More than you now have."

"Yes," said Frank. "Of course."

"So, let's…," Jonathan stopped in mid-sentence and looked to his left and noticed Frank's daughter Jennifer coming into the dining room through the kitchen door. Jonathan motioned to her to come to the table.

"You're Frank's daughter," Jonathan said.

"Yes, I'm Jennifer," said Jennifer.

"I'm Jonathan and I'm about to help your father with something, and if you would like, you can sit in and see if you agree with me."

"I'd love to," said Jennifer.

Jennifer took a seat next to her father. Jonathan stood as she sat down, and then sat back down himself. Frank's eyes smiled their approval at this old world gesture of courtesy. Jonathan looked at Jennifer.

"Your dad tells me that you've spent a lot of money on advertising, and that your ad reps are selling you on the idea of repetition, and getting your name out, and all of that. And I don't have to ask you whether these ads are effective because I come into this restaurant a lot and I can see with my own eyes that they are not."

"True," said Jennifer. "Thank you. I've been trying to tell my father that myself. As nice as he thinks that Rhiannon is from the paper, our ads really don't seem to be working…."

"Jennifer!" said Frank. "That's because we have not run them long enough. That's why we applied for the loan, so we could run through the rest of the year. Rhiannon and my radio people said this, too, that you have to have constant… constantness…consistency! And repeat and repeat before people will have it sink in."

Jennifer looked at her father and then looked at Jonathan. Jonathan waited a minute until he thought Frank was finished.

"Let me ask you something," said Jonathan, looking first at Frank but including both father and daughter. "What part of town do you live in? Or better, what direction do you drive into work in?"

"We come from the north side, down Winslow Avenue," said Jennifer.

"Okay," said Jonathan. "That's how I come here, too. There's a bar and grille a few blocks away on your way in here called The Bashful Bandit. Have you ever seen it?"

"How could you miss it?" laughed Jennifer. "It has one of those old signs that were put up in the 1950s and now they're grandfathered against the zoning laws and so it's huge, so how could we miss it?"

"How do you like the bar?" said Jonathan.

"I've never been in it," said Frank, and Jennifer shook her head, too, to indicate that she hadn't, either.

"Why not? Don't you ever go to a bar and grille?"

"Oh, yes," they both said together.

"We have our favorites," said Jennifer. "Polanski's, for one, and Dad likes a couple of the sports bars outside of Detroit."

"But you see the Bashful Bandit sign every day," said Jonathan. "The Bashful Bandit has more repetition and name I.D. than any other bar and grille in the world to the two of you, and you've never tried it even once?"

"Well...." said Frank, not quite buying the comparison.

"Okay then," said Jonathan. "What about Jack in the Box down the road? Do the two of you ever go there?"

"No," said Frank, looking disgusted. "We are in the restaurant business. We love good food. We would not go there."

"How do you know what kind of food they have if you don't go there?" said Jonathan.

"Oh, all the commercials on TV!" said Frank.

"They're everywhere," said Jennifer. "TV, billboards, radio... and I like the ads, that guy Jack is hilarious. Did you see the one where his son is playing football and he has to wear this huge helmet? Their ads are great."

"But you don't go there," said Jonathan.

"No," said Jennifer.

"Why not?" asked Jonathan.

"We don't have any reason to go there," said Jennifer. "We both cook, we both like great food, and we want to be healthy, too. Like I said, there's no reason for us to go to Jack in the Box."

"There you go," said Jonathan pushing his chair back a little from the table. "There you go."

There was silence. Frank looked puzzled, and Jennifer looked intrigued. Jonathan took a sip of his coffee and waited.

"No reason," Jonathan said.

"What do you mean by that?" said Jennifer.

Jonathan said, "Jack in the Box can run the best ads in the history of TV but if they can't give you a *reason* to go there, you won't. The Bashful Bandit can be a huge sign you see every day, but if they don't give you a reason to go there, you won't."

Jonathan looked over at the young waiter who was starting to take the cloths off the tables and set the chairs aside for the night's floor cleaning. "Oh, gosh," he said. "It looks like I'm in here after closing time."

"Okay, but wait!" said Frank. "I don't have this lesson yet. What do you mean 'no reason'?"

"Your ads give people no reason to come in," said Jonathan. "I don't have to look at your ads for the Sunshine Inn to know this. If they are not attracting people into your restaurant it's because they are not giving people a reason to come in. Repeating your name is not enough. Knowing the name doesn't give you a reason to come in. You have to give people a reason. Repetition means nothing. Name I.D. and getting your name out are of no value to you, Frank. You can see that. You can see it by the empty tables in here."

"Rhiannon says not enough repetition...." Frank said.

"Daddy, stop. Rhiannon has taken so much of your money you need a bank loan," said Jennifer. "And your radio reps are doing the same. This man is making sense, isn't he? People don't go places just because they know the name."

Frank gave a big sigh and pushed back from the table.

"So now you tell us," said Frank. "Now that it's too late. What can we do? Even if we learned how to make ads that gave people a reason to come in, it's too late, now. We are out of money. We are in trouble."

"You can do it without money," said Jonathan. "You can get it started without spending any significant money at all. Can you afford to print some flyers?"

"Of course," said Frank. "Or, I should say, maybe."

"Good," said Jonathan, "We'll continue to talk about this. But for now I have to run. My wife's out of town but I have some work to finish at home tonight. How about next Tuesday? I'll come in for lunch and if the two of you can meet me here, I'll show you an idea or two."

"What does a music teacher know?" said Frank.

"Daddy!" said Jennifer.

"I am so sorry," said Frank. "Forgive me. I am just so worried."

"We've got nothing to lose, Daddy," said Jennifer.

Jonathan extended his hand to her and shook it. Then he shook Frank's hand and smiled at him.

"Smile, Frank," said Jonathan. "We're about to let the sun shine in."

Chapter 4

Jonathan's faded blue Detroit Tigers baseball cap was pulled low on his head as he hopped from his old red Ferrari and walked through the strip mall parking lot to the Sunshine Inn on a bright Saturday morning. He was dressed in long, baggy, jeans shorts and a faded work shirt, and as he pushed through the door into the restaurant, he took off his cap and put it in his back pocket.

Except for what seemed like an entire girls' softball team seated by the front window, the restaurant was empty except for Frank's daughter Jennifer, who was at a far back table with school books and notebooks spread out in front of her and a pitcher of tea in the corner.

Jonathan smiled at her and she motioned him over to join her.

"Can you join me for a minute?" asked Jennifer, as she started to clear her books away. "We got your message about lunch last Tuesday...."

"I am so sorry," said Jonathan. "I was called out of the country on a business matter...." He pulled up a chair and sat at Jennifer's table.

"Out of the *country*?" said Jennifer. "You seem pretty busy for a music teacher."

"Yes, well, there are things other than music that I am working on, but bring me up to date on the restaurant and you and Frank."

"Well, my father's been pretty hard to handle since you left," said Jennifer, with a smile. "He wants to believe you can help us, but then he gets angry and wants to close the place down."

"And what do you want?" asked Jonathan.

Jennifer didn't know how to respond. She admired this young music teacher very much, and was intrigued by what he had to say. There was something about his logic that seemed even more informed than her marketing classes at Wayne State, which she thought were business theories taught by older men who never ran a business. Rather than argue with them, she memorized their opinions and fed them back to them on the exams. Her goal was the degree, not to revolutionize Wayne State.

"What do I want?" said Jennifer. "I want my father to be able to cook. That's his love. He would die a happy man if he could just cook for people and not worry about the business side of this business."

"Well, that's one of the problems here," said Jonathan. "You and your father see the 'business side' of this business as some separate, distasteful side that has to be dealt with. You'll never succeed that way."

"What do you mean by that?" asked Jennifer. "Surely you don't recommend that we ignore the business side and just stay in the kitchen and cook."

"In a way, yes, I do! And it took me years to learn this myself, so please don't think I'm lecturing you about anything. What I'm about to tell you is never learned by most business people, which is why four out of five small businesses go right out of business. They go right under."

"You don't look old enough to have years of experience learning anything," Jennifer said quickly but then wished she hadn't. It was too flirtatious, although she didn't mean it that way.

"I have failed miserably!" laughed Jonathan. "More than once, too! Total, crashing, flaming failures. Complete disasters. Something I wouldn't wish on anyone."

"And from that you concluded that we should just cook," said Jennifer.

"Yes, and here's what I mean by that. When Frank cooks, he is in creative control. He is clear and present, and he doesn't let any circumstance stop him from being great."

"That's really true," said Jennifer. "One night last year he ran out of ground beef and made a customer a fried portabella mushroom burger that was so good that it's now one of the most popular items on the menu! And he just improvised."

"Hey, I *love* that burger!" said Jonathan. "It's 'The Porta Prince,' right? Marinated in Italian dressing and charbroiled with a plum tomato and cheddar served with pasta on the side. I've brought people in for that one. He just made that up one day?"

"He's always doing that," said Jennifer. "Nothing fazes him. One day a customer ordered a strange kind of non-alcoholic beer and Frank didn't have it but he ran…literally *ran* out the back door to the Kroger's down the street and bought a six-pack of it and emerged from the kitchen a few minutes later with the beer for his customer."

Jonathan pulled his chair closer to the table and smiled. Any doubt he might have had about teaching these good people how to turn their restaurant around had completely disappeared. This inner quality that Frank had developed in the category of cooking was exactly what the "business side" needed, and Jonathan now knew he had something to work with.

"I can't tell you how happy you have just made me," said Jonathan. "This is the connection we will make with Frank. Yes, to answer your question, all we need to do to save this business is *cook*."

"Sounds too good to be true," said Jennifer.

"Which is why four business people out of five don't make it," said Jonathan.

"What's the connection there?"

"Well the fact that there is a guaranteed way to make your business succeed sounds too good to be true, so people dismiss the idea and go back to the easier way…."

"Which is?" asked Jennifer.

"Suffering," said Jonathan.

"Suffering?" laughed Jennifer as she poured herself half a glass of iced tea and pushed her chair back from the table, as if to distance herself from the craziness she was hearing.

Jonathan said, "Suffering! Worrying, fretting, complaining, problem-solving, coping, hoping…it's all suffering."

"Suffering is easy?"

"Easiest thing humans do," said Jonathan. "It takes no courage…no imagination…no energy…no integrity…anyone can do it, and that's why it's so popular. It's the path of least resistance.

The road most traveled. And the bonus is, you get pity. Miles and miles of sympathy from other sufferers. Just walk into any bar and listen for a while."

"Okay, I agree, that's the popular way to go into business for yourself, but what's the 'road less traveled' that successful people take?"

"Taking responsibility for creating and producing results," said Jonathan. "Taking full responsibility for your financial success. Full responsibility. Which means seeing yourself as the creator of your wealth...not some lucky circumstance."

Jennifer nodded cautiously, not at all bought in, or even fully understanding what this young man was talking about. She reached down to the chair next to hers and pulled a newspaper up and began to look through it while holding a finger up to Jonathan to keep his attention.

"Wait a minute," she said. "Let me show you something."

She paged through the paper and stopped and folded it into quarters and handed the folded paper to Jonathan pointing at the ad in the upper right-hand corner. Jonathan looked at the ad and shook his head.

THE SUNSHINE INN
Royal Oak's Best Restaurant
Best Food, Best Prices!

"May I have this ad?" Jonathan asked.

"Of course," said Jennifer. "I only show it to you because you talked about producing results. How can we take full responsibility for producing results when you never know what an ad like this will do? Even my professors at Wayne say you have to use repetition and establish your brand with your advertising. But that sounds so vague. Yesterday our class read a quote from a top advertiser in the corporate world who said, 'Half of my advertising budget is wasted money that brings no results; the problem is I don't know which half!'"

"That's a famous quote," said Sam. "But it should not be true. You should know exactly what your advertising is doing. Another famous quote, and a more accurate and useful one says,

'Advertising is *salesmanship in print*.' That's the quote you want to live by. If your sales person isn't selling, you get one who will. And you should take full responsibility for the results your advertising gets."

Jonathan began to get up from his seat.

Jennifer looked surprised and said, "Wait! You didn't order anything! I'm so sorry I took all your time talking about the business. Please sit down."

"I can't right now, I have to go somewhere. What we were talking about reminded me of something I want to show you and Frank…and I don't want to continue this until Frank is here. When can I meet with you both?"

"He's cooking now. Can you come in tonight at closing?"

"That's 10, isn't it?"

"Yes."

"Perfect. I'll be here."

"By the way," said Jennifer.

"Yes?" said Jonathan as he headed for the door.

"Where are you going so fast?"

"A toy store," said Jonathan.

Chapter 5

The dim stars were hung high in the muggy cool Michigan sky as Jonathan's 308 GTS engine rumbled to a stop in the parking lot outside the restaurant. Jonathan gave himself a minute to think about what a night like this in Hawaii would be like, were he really Magnum, and were there real criminal detective work to be done.

As he reached into the back seat for the plastic toy store bag it occurred to him that in some ways he was better than a detective. His life was more fun, not less. The world of business intrigued him so much that when he saw a challenge like Frank and Jennifer's restaurant, it was like a crime was being committed. It was a crime that such a good restaurant was going to have to close down. Jonathan knew it was happening to good businesses everywhere: People who knew their product but couldn't solve "the business side" of business.

Jonathan allowed himself a momentary daydreaming indulgence. Maybe he was just like his hero played by Tom Selleck on the old TV series. Thank goodness it was still being run on cable every night. What was it about that show that Jonathan liked so much? Hawaii was great, the car was great, and Selleck was just cool.

Jennifer was looking out of the front window of the restaurant, turning the sign from OPEN to CLOSED when she saw Jonathan standing by his car, running his fingers along the door and looking up at the night sky. Jennifer watched him for a minute and wondered who this interesting young man was who had taken such an interest in their restaurant. Her father told her he had gone to Jonathan's music studio to check him out and they said he had an office in Detroit. That was interesting. Then he has to leave the country? How could a music teacher have business in another country?

"Jennifer, what are you staring at?" called Frank from the opening to the kitchen.

"I'm just letting our music teacher in," she called back in a voice just a little too loud as she opened the door to Jonathan.

"It can be 'Jonathan,'" said Jonathan.

"What?" said Jennifer, smiling at him and looking at his toy store bag.

"Jonathan is what you can call me," Jonathan said.

Frank yelled out from the kitchen, "I'll just be a few minutes straightening up back here. We do the full kitchen cleaning early in the morning, but I get things straight for them."

"Can we join you?" called Jonathan.

"Sure," said Frank, and he smiled and waved them both to come into the kitchen.

As he put his last large pot into the sink, Frank turned to Jonathan and said, "Sir, I am afraid we must stop this meeting with you."

"Why is that?" asked Jonathan.

"You give us hope, then we argue, then we feel even worse, then we want to close everything down and the confusion gets worse every day. Today we had a very good day. But tomorrow? Tomorrow we may have nobody! Nobody! How can I know? Most days are bad."

"Frank, let me ask you something, if I may," said Jonathan, setting his plastic toy store bag on a metal table by the sink. Jennifer pulled up a high stool to sit on and Frank pulled off his apron and leaned against the sink, shrugging his shoulders and heaving a mild sigh, not altogether exasperated. He even looked a little friendlier around the eyes as he looked at this young man. *He is consistent*, thought Frank. *Or is it "persistent"? He is like me. When I was young. Not to be stopped. I like him. But does he know what he's talking about? His music studio looked beautiful, set back under those huge trees at the end of the road. It looked like a school building in England, like in that old movie I see on late night black and white TV..... "Goodbye Mr. Chips"? So he must have success. And an office in Detroit? I wonder what that office looks like.* "What do you wish to ask me?" Frank said, finally.

"When you cook, and you want to create a new dish for the menu, do you always get what you want the first try?"

Frank stared for a minute, and then started laughing.

"Should I tell you?" he asked. "Should I hurt my reputation with you? My only customer? Some days...yes!...my only customer! Should I now admit all kinds of mistakes?"

"One woman had to be taken to the hospital...." said Jennifer.

"Jennifer!" shouted Frank. "Not true! Not true that it was the cooking. She was crazy, and she had an allergy to shrimp."

Jonathan looked at Jennifer and saw that they both wanted to laugh more than they were.

Frank said, "Look. I make mistakes. But I am like Edison. Ten thousand mistakes. Ten thousand times Edison tries to make a light bulb, not making one, and finally he succeeds. I am sometimes like Edison. Sometimes I even go to his shop and look at his workplace."

Jonathan knew that Frank was referring to Greenfield Village not far down the road in Dearborn, where Edison's entire home and workplace were preserved at the open-air walk-around museum.

"Frank, that's what I hoped you would say," said Jonathan. "Because we are going to look at your whole business that way, like something you are going to cook and prepare...not some alien nightmare that you can't understand."

"Business is hard," said Frank.

"As hard as you think it is," said Jonathan.

"What's in your bag?" asked Jennifer, no longer able to restrain her curiosity. All three looked at the plastic toy store bag on the table. Jonathan pulled the bag from the table and looked around the floor.

"How many doors out of here?" he asked. "How many ways out of the kitchen?"

Frank looked confused. He said, "Well just that one that opens to the dining room, unless you mean the back door, too, we have a back door."

"Let's leave the back door closed," said Jonathan. "Let's just say that the front opening to the dining area is the only door out, okay? Can I prop a chair there to keep it open?"

Jennifer and Frank looked at each other and nodded and shrugged, willing to go along with whatever this was.

Jonathan got down on the floor. He perched on his knees and smiled back up at Jennifer and Frank.

"Here's our demonstration," said Jonathan as he pulled a toy out of his bag and began to wind it up. The toy was a little chick, a bright yellow and red metallic baby chicken. On the front beak was a plastic knob that looked like it was retractable. When Jonathan was finished winding up the chick he placed it on the floor of the kitchen and all three people watched it head for the wall, rolling along on little wheels beneath its feet. When the chick hit the wall, it turned slightly and rolled again and hit the baseboard, and turned again, and soon it was rolling across the floor until it hit the next wall. It turned again and rolled again and after about three minutes of hitting and turning it found its way out into the dining area at which point Jonathan jumped up and cheered.

"Freedom!" shouted Jonathan. "Success! It found its way out!"

Frank and Jennifer stared at him without saying anything.

"What is the mystery?" asked Frank. "It has a...how do you call it...a sensing?"

"A sensor," said Jennifer. "A sensing knob on the beak so when it hits anything it turns and keeps going."

"Exactly," said Jonathan, as if that rested his case.

"Are you...may I say it...toying with us?" asked Jennifer. "How does this apply to saving the restaurant?"

"It's the whole answer," said Jonathan. "It's what Frank does when he cooks. It's what you probably do with your studies. It's what everybody does with something they are good at or love doing. They don't stop. They turn and go again, turn and go again. Nothing stops them until they find what works. They're like Edison."

"How does that fit our business?" Frank asked.

"Well, in your business, you just stop," said Jonathan. "Or you hit the same wall over and over. Like your advertising. You hit the wall when an ad doesn't work, and you don't turn like the toy, you just keep hitting the same wall. You are not committed to having your advertising be as good as your cooking. You allow it to be a mystery. You allow other people to tell you things about it without trying things out for yourself."

"We don't turn," said Jennifer, starting to get excited. "We hit the wall a few times and wind down and quit."

"Right!" said Jonathan.

"Well, what kind of advertising works?" asked Frank.

"Not so fast," said Jonathan. "It's not that simple. The toy chick took a while to find the dining room. You might not use advertising at all…not like you think of it. Maybe the question is about communication. Getting your story out there. We don't know for sure, but until the two of you are willing to look at your business, the 'business side' of your business, with the same curiosity and passion you put into your cooking and your school studies, this place is going to be a broken toy."

"I see this!" shouted Jennifer, "Do you see this, Daddy?"

"Maybe I see this," said Frank. "But I still don't know how to love business as much as I love to cook."

"You must learn to," said Jonathan. "Just like you learned to cook. Did you always love cooking?"

"No!" said Frank. "I hated it! I was so frustrated, burning things, ruining things. But soon it became my love. The more I did it, the more I loved it."

"So let's start turning our love and attention to the one thing and the only thing that will save this business," said Jonathan. "You have to figure out what that one thing is, and then know it."

"Oh, I know what that is!" said Frank.

"Tell me," said Jonathan.

"Money!" said Frank.

"No," said Jonathan. "Not money. Something much more important to your business than money."

Jennifer looked puzzled and Frank looked stumped. Jonathan smiled at them and tilted his head questioningly, as if inviting them to think of the answer.

"Give us a clue," said Jennifer.

"Starts with a C," said Jonathan.

"Cash!" said Frank.

"Daddy, stop," said Jennifer. "It's the customer, right?"

"You just got your degree," said Jonathan. "And the next time we meet, we're going to prepare a recipe for bringing in the customer. We're going to cook it up, with mental persistence."

Frank shook his head and began turning off the lights in the kitchen.

"I wish I could believe you," he said.

"You don't have to," said Jonathan.

"What do you mean?" said Frank.

"Do you have to believe in gravity to have it work?" said Jonathan. "Do you have to believe a plane will fly to take a flight to Chicago? What I am going to show you is a business principle that works whether you believe in it or not."

They were standing in the dark. The sound of traffic outside was the only noise to be heard. Jennifer went into the dining area, followed by Jonathan.

"Let me get your toy for you," she said, "and I can't tell you how much I want to thank you for what you're doing, and, more than that, how you're doing it. No matter what he says, my father is starting to see this."

"I know he is," said Jonathan. "And let's keep the toy here. It will come in handy for the big event."

"What big event?" Jennifer said as she opened the front door for Jonathan.

"Your grand opening," said Jonathan.

"We had that eight years ago," she said.

"That's what you think," said Jonathan.

Chapter 6

Jonathan saw the police car right away. It was parked right in front of the entrance of The Sunshine Inn, and for a minute Jonathan's pulse skipped a beat but then he restored himself to sanity by thinking that cops knew where the good food was. Trust a cop to eat at the right place.

He got out of his car and walked to the restaurant and saw with satisfaction that the Inn was half-full today, and as he took a seat by the front window he heard his name.

"Jonathan," stage-whispered Jennifer as she hurried toward his table. "We have a problem."

"What is it?"

"We were robbed last night. The whole safe was taken out."

"Where's Frank?"

"He's in the back with the police, and I'm cooking today so I have to get back to the kitchen, but I think Frank could use a friend right now. This was not good timing, considering everything we're facing."

Jonathan nodded and said, "Tell Frank I'm here, and when he's through with the police I'll come back to talk to him."

"Thank you so much!" said Jennifer who turned and hurried back to the kitchen.

Jonathan grabbed a menu and when the waitress came to his table he ordered the raspberry iced tea and "Frank's Famous Red Wings" named after the sauce he invented for them and his favorite hockey team. The waitress brought him the tea right away, and Jonathan put a few drops of honey in it and stirred.

Why does the universe do this to people? Jonathan thought deeply as he sipped his tea. But then he corrected his course of thinking. *No*, he thought, *that's not it. There's a better way to see this: What is the universe trying to reveal here? Where's the gift inside this problem?*

Jonathan had learned to change the course of his thinking after a number of his own businesses failed in part because he wasn't learning the lessons that problems were trying to teach him. He was letting problems depress him and waste his energy on self-pity. Once he learned about the power he had to generate positive solutions by looking for the gift inside each problem, he began to succeed. That's what he wanted to show Frank and Jennifer how to do.

"One medium order of Red Wings?" the young waitress said to Jonathan as she stopped at his table.

"That's it!" said Jonathan. "And it looks like you have a little trouble today?" he added with a nod to the car outside the window that said "Royal Oak Police" on the door.

"We were robbed," said the waitress in a lower tone. "I know you're a friend of Frank's, so I can tell you."

"When did it happen?" asked Jonathan.

"Well, that's the problem," she said. "By the way, my name's Kelly—and that's...I mean that's the problem. No alarm went off. No signs of a break-in. They think it was one of us...or, I mean, someone who works here."

"Do you believe that?"

"Well, I don't know...Juwan has been acting weird lately, and Frank gave him a key, which I thought was a mistake, but Frank wanted him to be able to come in early and clean...."

"Juwan?"

"You've seen Juwan, he's the young black...African American guy...."

"Oh, yes," said Jonathan. "He's a nice guy. He seems like a good guy...I can't picture him...."

"Well, I couldn't either but lately he's been calling in sick a lot and, well just acting weird, but...hey, I've got to get busy," said Kelly as she turned toward a table that was calling to her.

"Thanks," said Jonathan nodding to her as she smiled back

at him.

Jonathan finished his wings and pulled a book from his pack to read while he ate. It was a tattered old copy of *I Don't Care If I Never Come Back* by Art Hill, the ultimate fan's book about baseball. Jonathan's ultimate dream was to own and run the Detroit Tigers someday, and he was getting closer to that dream than anyone connected to The Sunshine Inn could have imagined. To the people here, he was a music teacher who had had some success with his studio and somehow derived some universal principles from the experience. Principles, thought Jonathan, that could also take the Tigers to the top of the baseball world if they were carefully applied.

Jonathan's thought train was interrupted by the jarring sight of a very large police officer emerging from the kitchen area with Frank following behind. The two walked out of the front door into the Royal Oak summer sunshine and Jonathan could see them standing by the police car, talking. Frank was sorrowfully shaking his head and the officer was nodding and talking to Frank like Frank wasn't understanding something he needed to understand. The officer got into his car and Frank nodded, then shrugged, then made a pantomime motion of shrugging his shoulders in hopeless desolation. Jonathan saw the officer shake his head and shout something as he pulled out of the parking lot, and Frank then gave a tentative wave to him. This did not look good, thought Jonathan. This did not look good.

Frank slowly came back into the restaurant and stopped at a table that had a family at it and talked and shrugged and gestured and waved and walked quickly back into the kitchen area.

Jonathan finished his next to last Red Wing and left a $20 bill on the table for the food and for Kelly and followed Frank into the back of the restaurant.

"Frank!" said Jonathan, catching Frank right before he went into his little office in the back corner of the kitchen. Frank looked up and looked surprised and then waved Jonathan to join him in the office.

"Take a seat," said Frank, pointing to a large recliner in the corner of the crowded little office. Jonathan noticed a framed photo of the Red Wings embracing the Stanley Cup. Under that photo was a signed photo of Joe DiMaggio. And next to that was a framed photo of a woman who looked like Anne Bancroft in *The Graduate*. Frank noticed that Jonathan was staring at the photo of the woman.

"Isabella," said Frank. "My wife. Does she look like Anne Bancroft to you?"

"Yes," said Jonathan.

"People all say that," said Frank. "She was my saint. But I'm ashamed to say I am almost happy she is gone right now."

"Why is that, Frank?"

"Because of this. All of this," said Frank as he pointed to papers on his desk that looked like a police report.

"What happened, Frank?"

"We were robbed. The safe, the whole safe was taken from my office," said Frank as he pointed to a corner where the safe had been. "A lot of cash, a lot of cash I had been saving for when we went out of business. People can't come get your cash like they can your bank account. A lot of cash and a lot of valuables like Isabella's jewels that I couldn't stand to keep at home and stock papers for Jennifer's schooling…."

"Those papers can be replaced," said Jonathan.

"But what can't be replaced is the trust," said Frank. "Someone I trusted robbed us."

"Do you know who?"

"I think it was Juwan, but I don't want to think that. I love that boy and he is so good, so smart and he has a good heart. He was in so much trouble when I hired him. He has no parents and he wanted to get out of his gang…."

"Okay, Frank, I hear you," said Jonathan. "But I think it is *you* who has a big heart, and there's nothing wrong with that unless you mix it up with your business. This is a *business*, Frank, not the Salvation Army. You have to respect it."

"I thought a job would help him, and we needed someone because our other clean-up man quit a week earlier and I was having to come in myself, and Juwan was the first person who applied and I knew he had some problems trying to get off drugs, but that was not his fault, that was the gang's fault."

"Frank, I don't fault you for wanting to help Juwan. And maybe we can still help Juwan. My own business partner, Mitch, has a real understanding of addiction and recovery, so I will ask him to help us if you still want to help Juwan."

"You would do that?"

"Yes, I will be glad to do that."

"So I need a new clean up person."

"True, and a safe-deposit *box* at the *bank* that's secure, not a little safe in your office."

"Show me how to do that."

"I will, but you must use this moment, this crisis, to your advantage."

Frank stared at Jonathan in disbelief. He looked offended.

Frank said, "Please, sir, do not mock me in my painful moment."

"Frank, I do not mock you. I honor you, but right here and right now there is something you can *get* like you never got before, if you're ready. Something you can understand. And if you get it, it will change your life and change this restaurant forever."

Frank stared at Jonathan for what seemed like three minutes and then pulled up his chair closer to the desk and said, "What is it?"

"The police think this is an inside job, right, Frank? They have no signs of a break-in. Whoever it was just took the safe and left. Right?"

"Right! Juwan!" said Frank. "I gave him a key. He didn't show up this morning."

"Right. True. But he's not the one who robbed you, Frank."

"What are you talking about?"

"He's not the one who robbed your restaurant."

"Who was it?"

"It was you, Frank. Even if it was Juwan, it was you. You robbed yourself, Frank. You stole from yourself today."

Frank just stared at Jonathan.

Jonathan said, "Frank, there is nothing wrong with this restaurant that you can't fix, because it has been *you* who has allowed it to break down. It's all you. You are the problem, Frank. The way you approach this restaurant, without strong, innovative business principles, letting your heart and your emotions rule everything you do, your relationship with your advertising girl, what is her name?..."

"Rhiannon."

"Rhiannon. Your emotional saving of Juwan, all of this at the expense of your restaurant, Frank."

"I am the problem?"

"Yes, Frank, you are the problem."

"So I should just close it down! Or sell it to someone who is not a problem."

"No, Frank. Wrong conclusion."

"Then what is the right conclusion? What is the solution?"

"You, Frank! Because if you are the problem, you are the solution! That's the good news. That's the gift you don't see. You are the solution."

"But how can I be the solution if I don't know what to do?"

"It's not really about doing, it's about being," said Jonathan. "You have to become as present to your business as you are to your cooking. That's the first step. You have to decide that you are going to make this work. That's what a commitment is, a decision. You decide to do it. To succeed at it. Not to survive it, but to succeed at it."

"Then what?

"Then you ask for help!" said Jonathan. "The first sign that a person is committed is that he asks for help."

"I thought that was a sign of weakness."

"It's the opposite, Frank. It's a sign that you care more about a result than you do about your self-image or your ego or whether you might lose face. Succeeding becomes your top priority, and you forget yourself in the name of making something happen...in your case, making the restaurant great. Absolutely great."

"Who will help me?"

"Jennifer can help you and I can help you but you have to ask for it and you have to choose to be committed to business excellence."

Frank got up from his desk and raised the shade on a very small window that looked out on the alley next to the restaurant. A little more light beamed through the window across his desk, landing on the police report.

"You don't understand how hard my life has been," said Frank.

"Everybody has a hard life, Frank. Everybody."

"Then why go on?"

"Because the sadness isn't real. It's just a bunch of emotions that get blocked in your body and mind and soon you take them for reality. You identify with them, but they are not you. They are just clouds. The earth doesn't identify with the clouds, it just lets them pass."

"What is real reality, then?"

"Joy," said Jonathan. "Curiosity. Energy. Invention. Frank's Porta Prince Mushroom Burger Delight! All the things you felt as a little boy, Frank. All those things you felt when you first opened your very own restaurant. You can get back to that again, and you can use this restaurant as a way to do it."

"Let me think about this," said Frank.

Jonathan stood up and looked again at the photo of the Red Wings and the Stanley Cup, then at the framed photos of DiMaggio and of Isabella. He looked down at the police report, and then looked up at Frank and extended his hand.

"I will not be coming in again, Frank," said Jonathan.

Frank said nothing.

Then Frank spoke, "I don't think I heard you right. What did you just say?"

"I will not be coming in again. I will not be available to talk to you again. This is our last talk. I cannot help you anymore, Frank, because I am not the solution. You are."

"You'll never come in again?" said Frank. "There goes half our business!" he laughed wildly, falsely, and then stopped and said, "I am kidding. And you are, too! Right? You are kidding."

"Frank, no. Until you make your commitment to succeed, I will not be coming back. I can't help you, and it would be too heartbreaking for me to come to a restaurant that is going under."

Jonathan turned to leave but was stopped by Frank's panicked voice.

"Wait! What if I decide to make this commitment, how will you know? How can I ask for your help if you don't come in?"

"If you're committed, you'll find me," said Jonathan.

"How will I find you? You are not at your music studio, I have been there."

"Committed people are very resourceful, Frank. Remember the wind-up toy? You'll find me, and you'll come to me. I won't come to you."

Jonathan turned and left and Frank sank more deeply into his chair, more despondent and depressed than ever. How dare that young man say I robbed myself? *How dare he leave us now? How can life get any worse than this?*

Chapter 7

Mary Kay Williams stood outside the front door of The Sunshine Inn with her soft leopard skin briefcase under one arm while she used the other hand to keep knocking. Even though the sign in the door said CLOSED Mary Kay knew she had an appointment with Frank to try to collect something on the growing advertising debt to her station, WFFM.

Finally the door opened, and it was Jennifer, not Frank, beckoning her inside and showing her a table by the front. Both young women sat down. There was a fresh pitcher of water with lime slices in it and Jennifer poured herself a glass and gestured toward the pitcher, but Mary Kay shook her head and opened her briefcase and took out a yellow legal pad for notes.

"Please excuse us," said Jennifer, "We're still a little behind things after the...incident."

"Frank told me," said Mary Kay. "And I'm really sorry about the robbery. Normally I wouldn't come at all, but you know. This has gotten so late and my own manager is on *me* about it and says it's my responsibility."

"I understand," said Jennifer. "I wish I had something to tell you, but we just don't have the money. It was all we could do to pay the mortgage on the building this month, and we're that close to closing the whole thing down."

"So, how do you do this?" said Mary Kay.

"Excuse me?" said Jennifer.

"How do you go to school full time and run the restaurant for your father?"

"Well, I don't run it," said Jennifer. "I just help out."

"Who runs it?" said Mary Kay.

"Frank has always run it," said Jennifer.

"Well, if it's about to go under, maybe you *should* run it," said Mary Kay. "Women are always better at this kind of thing anyway."

Jennifer said nothing.

Mary Kay said, "Okay, here is our final offer before we take you to collections. You pay half of what you owe us by Wednesday, that's two days from today, and we'll let you keep running your jingle and your spot if you make payments of at least a thousand dollars a week after that until we're brought current."

Jennifer looked over at the leopard-skin briefcase and then back at Mary Kay's hopeful face.

"No," said Jennifer. "I appreciate your offer, but no."

"Jennifer, I'm giving you a way to keep running your ad."

"And what good would that do? Why would that do anything more than run us deeper into debt with you?"

"So…you're going with another station? I wouldn't if I were you. Because if you don't take this offer I can promise you that we will put the word out on the street that you're bad credit. The word will go out to the other media."

"Mary Kay, let's be very clear. The advertising has simply not worked for us. I realize that we owe you money, but we aren't getting any more customers in than when we didn't advertise."

"That's because you don't advertise enough," said Mary Kay. "You need to build your brand. You need repetition and name ID. You need to get the word out because people just don't know about you yet."

"And when would that happen?"

"You reach a tipping point," said Mary Kay. "One day you reach a kind of critical mass."

Jennifer laughed. "It's critical already, Mary Kay, and I'm ready to start going back to Mass, and you've been saying this for over half a year, now. You have charmed my father and he thinks you're wonderful, but we simply won't do something that doesn't work."

"Then you haven't taken Advertising and Marketing 101 at Wayne State?"

"What do you mean by that remark?"

"Well, if you learned anything at Wayne State you'd learn that advertising takes time. You have to build share of mind. You have to position yourself for brand equity."

"I've read all that," said Jennifer. "And that all sounds intelligent, but right here right now we are dealing with *reality*, Mary Kay, and we have a great restaurant and very few customers."

"Fine!" said Mary Kay, collecting her pen and pad and putting them in her soft briefcase. "Fine. Then you'll be hearing from our attorneys."

"Send them over; we'll fix them a good meal."

"I don't think humor is very appropriate right now, Jennifer. You're looking at serious legal action. And on a personal note, I don't appreciate not collecting commission on all the work I've done."

"You've done some work on my father, that's for sure."

"Well, if you think that's true, then why do you let him make those decisions?"

Jennifer stared at Mary Kay, about to shoot a cutting answer back, but then thinking differently.

"Tell me again what you just said," said Jennifer, softly now.

"Well, I'm just saying you're a grown-up, Jennifer, and so is your father. And you're the business major in college. I don't buy it that you are innocents, little lambs from the old country being taken advantage of by the wicked radio reps. That story might work for you, but it doesn't work for me. Someone has to step up here, Jennifer. You're not just daddy's little girl anymore, you're a grown woman and if you don't think he's doing the right thing, then pay your debts and mend your ways and grow up."

Jennifer slouched back in her chair as Mary Kay stood to leave.

Mary Kay said, "Oh, don't bother to get up, I know the way out."

As the bells on the door jingled as Mary Kay left, Jennifer looked outside to see the ivory-colored Lexus she was getting into. She's not hurting for commissions, thought Jennifer, but she's right about everything else she said. I can't hide behind "I'm just a student" anymore, or "I'm daddy's little girl" anymore. I myself have to make a decision, here. This feels like one of those crossroad moments. I need to make a choice.

Jennifer found herself wondering what the music teacher would say.

Chapter 8

Jonathan loved driving the Ferrari with the top removed and so did his longtime canine companion Higgins, whose white, black and brown beagle ears always twisted in the wind as the classic car flew down the back roads of Michigan.

He'd had a few days to think since his confrontation with Frank in the back office of the restaurant, and he decided that he had no attachment to any particular outcome. If Frank didn't have the heart or the will to make his restaurant a success, he wasn't going to waste any more time with him. If, on the other hand, there was still some fire in Frank, then he was ready to help.

So when he got the call from Frank's daughter Jennifer this morning, he was only half surprised. First, because it was her and not Frank, and second because she wanted to meet with him right away about some conversation she had with a radio rep. Jonathan explained that he was not coming into the restaurant anymore, so they arranged to meet elsewhere.

He pulled into the parking lot of the Cranbrook Art Museum, the mutual site they had chosen. When Jennifer called, Jonathan had said "I have to walk Higgins this morning," and Jennifer immediately said, "Good, I'll join you. I feel like I have to talk to you."

Jonathan got out of his 308 GTS and attached the leash to Higgins who was almost too excited to bear the prospect of a walk down by the lake near the gallery.

Jonathan looked up to see that Jennifer was pulling up in Frank's old truck. Jennifer broke into a huge smile when she saw the little beagle straining to run at the end of Jonathan's leash. Jennifer stepped down from the truck and walked up to the man and his little dog.

"So this is Higgins," said Jennifer.

"This is the little man himself," said Jonathan, watching as Jennifer fell to her knees to play with Higgins and scratch him behind his ears. The little dog Higgins could tell right away that Jennifer was an "animal person," and became so involved with her that he momentarily forgot his run.

"Shall we walk?" said Jonathan. All three set out toward the lake and the many trees that hung over the water.

"I know what you told Frank," said Jennifer. "About making a decision. Making a commitment."

"Right," said Jonathan.

"It took him a long time to let that sink in," she said. "I mean, it was really hard for him. He thought you were blaming him for the robbery and all the hard times we've had, and he was furious about that for a while."

"I wasn't blaming him so much as showing him his accountability in all of it, his responsibility," said Jonathan. "How he co-creates his reality then pretends it just happens to him."

"Yes! I see that! And I…for a while I couldn't see it at all. When he told me about your conversation with him I was angry with you. I thought you were hitting a poor old man while he was at his lowest."

"I can see where it would seem like that. So what happened? How did you come to see it differently?"

"I was with that radio sales person Mary Kay Williams, and she was trying to collect money and run more ads, if you can believe it, and she got all hissied up when I told her we couldn't pay right now, and she came down on me pretty hard about my own responsibility in all of this."

"How did you feel about that?" said Jonathan.

"Well, it was amazing," said Jennifer, "I started to get angry and wanted to make it all be about how she had taken advantage of my father with her flirtatious sales techniques and marketing mumbo jumbo about branding and repetition, but it was like suddenly a new thought came to me and I could see this light...or something like that. The truth just hit me."

"Which truth was that?"

"She was right! She was so right," said Jennifer. "Oh, not about the repetition or running that insane jingle any more times, but about my needing to grow up and take some responsibility in this."

Jonathan stopped walking for a moment to look at Jennifer.

Jennifer said, "So I dropped out of school yesterday. Or at least I filed for the forms to do it."

Jonathan tried to see what was in her eyes. They seemed to have some hopeful light in them. Jonathan then kneeled down to take the leash off of Higgins.

"Stay on shore, Higgins, stay by the shore line," he said as Higgins burst like a bullet toward two swans that were on the edge of the lake. The swans lazily took flight, but not before they'd let Higgins get tantalizingly close.

"Tell me exactly why you dropped out of college," said Jonathan.

"I want to make the *restaurant* my school!" said Jennifer. "My senior class project. My real life business lab, whatever. I want to roll up my sleeves and learn business from the front lines, not in some classroom with old men teaching old theories."

"Wayne State is a good school," said Jonathan.

"But it's a school," said Jennifer. "That's the whole point. It is a school. It is not reality, and I want to engage reality. I realized that I'd been hiding from reality, I'd been playing daddy's little girl all my life, and now I was playing *I'm just a student don't blame me I just try to help out here.*"

"And that was a game?"

"Of course."

"Just an act?"

"Yes, just an act. Don't you believe me?"

"I just want to see if *you* believe you," said Jonathan.

They walked by the edge of the lake with Higgins running up to them and then running away again when they reached down for him. There was something happy about this moment for all three in the trio.

"I'd like to help you, but we need Frank, too," said Jonathan.

"Frank will come around," said Jennifer. "He hit the ceiling when I told him I'd dropped out. He walked out of the restaurant. But Frank's very emotional. He's old country, in case you hadn't noticed. He will come around."

"I told him he had to find me, that he had to seek me out for me to help you," said Jonathan.

"Oh, I know that," said Jennifer. "Believe me; he told me the whole story. He gave me your whole exchange. More than once. But I'm confident and I've seen a little sign."

"A little sign?"

"This morning when I was in his office getting the keys to the truck, the phone book was open to Music Schools and a black pen had circled the 'House of Harmony' Corporate office in Detroit."

"That's a good little sign," said Jonathan with a smile.

Higgins was now halfway around the lake and Jonathan cupped his hand and gave a piercing whistle, which caused Higgins to stop in his tracks and then come running back.

"He obeys you?" said Jennifer.

"Of course not," said Jonathan.

"Then why did he come running?"

"He associates it with food."

"Manipulator."

"Exactly."

"So what's next? I know I can't pay you, but I also know that you can help us. What do you think I should do next?"

"Well, you just go to that red car and get the plastic bag of biscuits in the front door pocket...."

"No! About the restaurant! You know what I'm talking about."

"I want you to rent a movie," said Jonathan.

"A movie?"

"Yes. I want you to rent a movie and watch it with Frank. That's all I want you to do. Once you've done that, and once Frank contacts me to say he's in, we'll proceed from there."

"What's the movie?" said Jennifer.

"*You've Got Mail,*" said Jonathan.

"The Tom Hanks movie?" said Jennifer.

"I've always thought of it as a Meg Ryan movie," said Jonathan.

"Hey…Mr. Married Man…."

"My wife looks just like Meg Ryan," said Jonathan.

"Nice save," said Jennifer.

"No, I'm not kidding."

"Well, why this particular movie?" said Jennifer.

"We'll talk after you see it," said Jonathan. "Is it a deal?"

Higgins was trying to get into the red Ferrari. Jennifer reached over the door and pulled out a baggie of biscuits.

"How many does he get?" said Jennifer.

"All of them," said Jonathan.

Chapter 9

Frank's house always brought a flood of childhood memories back to Jennifer. It was at the end of a tree-lined, leafy, shadowy Royal Oak neighborhood that made her think of Hansel and Gretel and people who lived in the forest. The sun came through to the street in shafts like in those hokey but beautiful Thomas Kinkade paintings, and driving into Frank's driveway gave Jennifer's heart a good, lonely feeling. This had been her mother's house, too.

"Ah, good!" Frank shouted when he opened the door and let Jennifer in, "and what is it you have brought?" looking down at the Blockbuster DVD Jennifer was holding.

"This is our movie for tonight," said Jennifer. "I told you all about it."

"Oh, but Jennifer, do we have to?" said Frank. "First we have toys and now a movie? All in the middle of such trouble."

"I trust him," said Jennifer. "And you know what the toy was about."

"Yes! It was about me!" said Frank. "How I run into walls and just stop."

"No, Daddy, it's not just about you, it's about me, too. I need to learn Don't-stop-till-you-find-your-way, too. That was for me, too."

Frank walked to the refrigerator and took out a pitcher of lemonade. He showed it to Jennifer and she nodded yes. Then she shook her head no.

"Do you have a beer?"

Frank set the lemonade down on the coffee table and went back to his refrigerator and pulled out a bottle of Rolling Rock for Jennifer.

Frank said, "So you stop school! You learn 'Don't-Stop' but you stop going to school. Wonderful."

"I have made a commitment to the restaurant. I can always finish school later. Unless I turn my full attention to this restaurant, it will go under. It may be too late, it may go under anyway, but I couldn't live with myself if I hadn't done this. And I know it was the best decision I've ever made."

"How do you know?" said Frank. "I wanted you to have a college education. I wanted to give that to you."

"You can give me more than that," said Jennifer. "You can give me your own commitment to the Inn. You can call Jonathan and get this turnaround started."

"I am trying, but it is too hard for me," said Frank.

Jennifer kneeled down to the DVD player under the TV and slipped the disc in and looked around for the remote.

"Okay," she said. "Let's watch this movie. I promised him we would."

"This is silly," said Frank.

"No," said Jennifer. "Do you know what's silly? Being a great cook with a good restaurant and going out of business is silly. Failure is silly. You know it."

Frank sat down in his favorite big chair and Jennifer stretched out on the couch as the movie credits came up and they began to watch together.

Tom Hanks and Meg Ryan were email buddies who met on the internet, and coincidentally they were both in the book business. They didn't know each others' real names, but came to enjoy and respect each others' thoughts via email. Meg owned a little bookstore that specialized in children's books and had been on the corner in the big city for two generations. Meg had all kinds of interesting activities for her customers, and had times when she would gather her customers' kids in a circle and read to them. She had a loyal following for her little bookstore and was happy until she heard that the big giant bookstore chain was opening a multistory store across the street. Tom Hanks was a senior executive in that big chain, although Meg didn't know that.

As the big chain store moves in to take over the neighborhood with bigger inventories and lower prices, Meg's store feels like it is being driven out of business. Meg gets upset and even organizes some street protests, like anti-war protests with angry signs and bullhorns! But the big store just moves right in and Meg closes her store. Romantically, the ending is a happy one, but for Meg's store the ending is depressing.

Frank and Jennifer watched in silence as the credits came up at the end. Jennifer thought, what in the *world* was the music teacher thinking? How could this depressing movie be any help to them at all? What was he wanting them to see?

Jennifer sat in gloomy silence as Frank got up to check the oven.

"What have you got in there?" Jennifer said. "It smells delicious!"

"Old country pizza," said Frank. "My way. Come to the dinner table."

"Look, I'm sorry about the movie," said Jennifer. "I have no idea...."

"Jennifer!" said Frank. "She quit!"

"Who quit?"

"Peg Ryan!"

"Meg."

"She quit!"

"Well, yes, because what choice did she have? I mean if you have a small bookstore, and some big national chain moves in...."

Frank cut slices from his pizza and they sat down at his small kitchen table. Pictures of Jennifer and her mother were displayed in order on the wall facing the table. Jennifer took a bite as stringy cheese dripped down to her plate. She looked warily at Frank, who was acting inappropriately happy about this sad movie.

"She didn't have to quit, Jen," said Frank. "That is the music teacher's point. She could have tried things and tried things, like cooking a new dish until you get it perfect, she could have done that."

"What about the competition?"

"What about when you run out of an ingredient? You invent! She could have had special offers for her customers. She could have done many more things like her reading groups. She said her mother owned the store for years and years. Think of all those customers! She could have had a customer thank you day every month…I am thinking all through this movie…everything the big store can't do, she could do…but she quit. She just quit. What did she try? Nothing!"

"So why does that make you happy?" said Jennifer.

"I see myself! I have quit! Look at the pictures, Jen! Look right there over your shoulder on the wall."

Jennifer looked up to see the photo gallery of herself at various stages of being a little girl with her mother and sometimes with a very happy Frank in the photos.

"Okay, I see Mom and me and you."

"What else do you see? Look in the eyes."

"I don't know what you want me to see."

"There is no quit in those eyes. In your mother's eyes or mine."

"And what does all this mean?"

"In the movie, when they are so in love at the end, I could see my life, Jen. I know when I quit. I quit when your mother died."

"But it was you who held us all together."

"But inside, I quit. I quit like that stupid Peg Ryan quit. No ingredients? Then I quit!"

"And this makes you happy."

"Look at your mother, Jen. She would not quit. She would not want the Sunshine Inn to quit. She would not want me to quit. I was using her. I was using her death to be in self-whatever you call it."

"Self-pity."

"Self-pity! Self-pity! I was using your mother for self-pity!"

"Dad, okay, okay, please calm down. Everybody grieves and…."

"Call the music teacher!"

"Dad, no."

"Why not!"

"He said you had to find him. You had to seek him out so he would know you'd made your decision."

"Give me your cell phone," said Frank.

"Why?" said Jennifer. "You have a phone here."

"You called him, no? You met him and talked to him about dropping out of college, no? His number is on your phone, find it and punch it for me."

"Wow, very resourceful, Dad."

Jennifer went to the living room where she had left her bag on the couch. Picking up her denim bag and pulling out her phone, she stopped for a second, remembering Mary Kay's leopard skin briefcase, and slowly she began to smile to herself. That moment with Mary Kay was like this moment must be for Frank, she thought.

"Punch it," said Frank.

Jennifer searched for Jonathan's number and punched it for Frank saying, "It's late. He won't be in that office now."

"I don't care," said Frank. "I will leave a message."

Jennifer saw Frank waiting through what must have been a long voice message and then heard him say, "Kind sir! Jona...Jonathan, sir. This is Frank Mills. The Sunshine Inn. I will not quit. Sir I will not...." and Frank could not continue. He opened his mouth to speak but a whisper was all he could do and the tears were really flowing now. Frank finally handed the phone to Jennifer as he sat down, drained of every ounce of energy. Jennifer stood beside him and held his shoulders as he shook with deep sobs.

"Dad, we're going to make this work."

Frank nodded his head in agreement as the crying started to fade away. Jennifer picked up her phone from where it had fallen to the floor and saw that the connection had been lost. She snapped it shut, put it in her bag and gave her father a final hug. She could sense that he wanted to be left alone in the house he used to share with her mother.

Frank walked Jennifer to the door and gave her a goodbye hug.

Jennifer said, "Bye, Dad."

"I should call him back?" said Frank. "I think I couldn't finish my message, so he won't get why...."

"No, no," said Jennifer. "He'll get it. He'll get the message. He'll come."

Chapter 10

Juwan Jefferson was arrested in his apartment on a Sunday morning while church bells sounded throughout East Detroit. The safe that he had taken from The Sunshine Inn was right there for the officers to see when they came in after flashing their badges at Juwan's terrified uncle.

"You make this too easy," said the big blonde officer when he saw the safe. The officer looked like he worked out with weights more than once a day. His partner, a small African American, put his arm around Juwan's uncle's shoulders and told him not to worry, he could sit down in the corner and they would handle everything from here.

Juwan looked almost grateful when they put the cuffs on his trembling wrists and led him down to the squad car. He could hear his uncle calling out, "It's the drugs! He's a good boy! They made him take the drugs."

As they rode through the burned-out, bombed out neighborhood that was home to Juwan, the blonde office looked back at Juwan through the safety mesh screen while his partner drove.

"Juwan, your uncle says someone made you take drugs," said the big blonde officer. "How exactly does that happen, Juwan, that someone can make you take drugs? I don't remember anybody making me take anything since I was a little, little boy. Are you a little boy, Juwan?"

His partner, who was driving, shot him a look and said, "That's enough, Blake! This will be done right, at the right time."

The blonde officer laughed and said to Juwan, "Oh you've got a friend, Juwan. Right here in this car! My partner here had a little addiction problem once, right Monroe? So you've got sympathy. Just what you need. Justice is too old fashioned, isn't it? You all need sympathy!"

Juwan sat in silence, still shaking and fighting back tears as the car drove on to the station.

The blonde cop, Blake, went on.

"And tell me this, Juwan, how stupid do those drugs make you? We found all the money you stole still there in the safe. How dumb a criminal do you have to be to steal money and then leave it in the safe you took, right out there open in your apartment?"

"I was going to return it," said Juwan, with a strained voice neither cop could hear.

"You were what?" shouted the blonde cop.

"Leave him alone," said the black cop at the wheel as they drove on in silence until he looked over at his white partner and said, "You know, Blake, you have been a good partner for me. You have saved my life...literally. But there's a lot you need to learn. I don't think you quite understand what it's like to crash...or detox, as they now call it. It's worse than anything you can imagine. There is a punishment right there in the drugs for the user. I have half a mind to shoot you up so you can get a little feel for what I'm saying."

Blake said nothing as the car pulled in to the station back parking lot. Monroe came around to guide Juwan out of the vehicle.

He said to him, "We're gonna get you booked, son, and then I'm going to talk to your uncle about what's next for you. There's something you gotta get here about life...you can't take what's not yours, I don't care how strung out you are. You're gonna pay for that and it's a good thing you are. You need a bottom to hit, and I hope this is it."

Juwan let the black cop pull him by the arm into the booking room and kept his head hung low.

"Is there anyone you want me to call for you?" said the cop.

"Call Frank," said Juwan. "Call my boss."

"Frank? He's the restaurant owner? I doubt if he's going to be happy to talk to you right now, Juwan. And I doubt if he's your boss any more, either. Just because the money's still there doesn't mean that you're not a criminal, and that he hasn't been robbed."

"Call him, tell him what has happened and tell him I am sorry."

"Okay, I'll see what I can do. I've got his number," said the officer. "And just tell me one more thing, just between you and me, what did your uncle mean about people making you take drugs?"

"My old gang," said Juwan. "It's been going on for years. I'm not with them but I haven't been able to quit the drugs. My uncle is confused. He thinks they still make me shoot up. Once they did, during initiation, but not for years."

"Can you give up some names for me?"

"They're gone," said Juwan. "They've been sent up. Most of them. You've heard of them...Lords of the 313."

"You were one of the freaking Lords of the 313?" said the officer.

"No, that's what my uncle was saying. I ran with them, I ran some stuff for them, and I got high and everything, and it became a nightmare. But I was never a 'member,' as you call it."

"I'm sorry this all had to happen," said the officer. "You need to see about getting yourself some help."

"No chance," said Juwan.

Chapter 11

Jonathan got Frank's broken-off message late on a Thursday night, and pulled his red Ferrari 308 GTS into the Sunshine Inn's parking lot on Saturday, two mornings later as they were opening for breakfast.

On the front seat in the car with him was the newspaper, folded in quarters, with the Sunshine Inn ad in the upper corner that said:

THE SUNSHINE INN
Royal Oak's Best Restaurant
Best Food, Best Prices!

In smaller print there were directions, a little map and a phone number, plus a quotation from *Detroit Today* magazine that said "The cooking of Frank Mills is the best-kept secret in the whole suburban Detroit area!"

No wonder it's a secret, thought Jonathan, as he glanced down at the ad while stopped in the parking lot. Underneath the folded newspaper on the seat Higgins usually rode in was a brightly-colored wooden Russian doll, the kind that opens to smaller and smaller dolls contained inside. Jonathan was a great believer in teaching tools.

Frank and Jennifer were seated at a back table in the restaurant when Jonathan walked in with his doll and the newspaper under one arm. They looked up, saw him and motioned him over to their table. Frank looked happier than Jonathan could remember seeing him in many months.

"Good morning!" said Frank as he stood to greet Jonathan and offer him a chair at the table. "You got my message."

"Yes," said Jonathan. "Yes, thank you, your message was loud and clear. No more discussion of commitment. You're in."

"Yes," said Frank. "And Jen has quit her school, which I don't like but...."

"...but you will," said Jonathan. "I have a friend at Apple—the big computer company?—who dropped out of college and said it was the best decision he ever made because it forced him to be innovative. He later created Pixar studios, the iPod...."

"Wait a minute," said Jennifer, "you're talking about Steven Jobs, the CEO and, like, *founder* of Apple, you *know* him?"

"We're not best buddies, but yes," said Jonathan.

"Both of you have lost me," said Frank. "I make a great apple cobbler, which you have ordered sir, more than once, but that is my knowledge of apples."

Frank looked happy and comfortable as he settled into his chair across from Jonathan.

"Aren't you cooking today, Frank?" said Jonathan.

"Breakfast, my cousin Vladek cooks," said Frank. "I save myself. And Jennifer said you were coming in, you left us a message, and so I am ready to work. To change. You want to order?"

"Yes, sure," said Jonathan.

Frank motioned for the young waitress with red hair in corn rows to come to the table, and Jonathan said, "I'll have two eggs basted, and sides of steamed spinach and smoked salmon with coffee."

"The usual for you," said Frank. "And I see you have some kind of doll with you."

Jonathan reached down and put his Russian doll up on the table. It was brightly painted and lacquered with red and yellow patterns of flowers on the dress of the woman whose shape the doll took.

"This is the doll I use when I talk about hiring," said Jonathan. "It has come in very handy for me."

"I know this doll from where I come from," said Frank.

"Frank grew up in Poland, Rumania and Italy before coming to this country," said Jennifer. Jonathan understood why he hadn't been able to pinpoint Frank's old world accent.

Frank said, "This doll is called a *matryoshka*. This means grandmother. You open her, and you find many more. You find her daughters and granddaughters inside."

Jonathan opened the doll to show that there was a slightly smaller, identical doll inside. He laid the shell of the bigger doll on the table and then opened the other doll to find a slightly smaller doll.

"I've always loved these dolls," said Jennifer. "Why did you bring this one?"

"This is how we're going to think about Juwan, and not just Juwan, but all your employees from now on," said Jonathan.

Jennifer looked puzzled, but pleasantly so. Frank began to suppress laughter.

"What's so funny?" said Jennifer.

Frank said, now laughing out loud, "Ingredients: One and one half ounce vodka, and three quarter ounce coffee flavor brandy! Black Russian. Maybe the music teacher says Juwan is a black Russian!"

"This has nothing to do with Juwan being black," said Jennifer. "Juwan was just released from jail, Dad. This is not something to joke about, really."

"Where is he now?" asked Jonathan.

"He's officially back at his apartment with his uncle, but he's actually attending a treatment program that one of the police officers got him into," said Jennifer. "We recovered everything. The safe, the money, the jewelry, everything."

"Okay, good, but let's look at what we lost," said Jonathan. Jennifer was pleased to hear him say "we."

"We lost a worker, I have to do it myself now while I look for someone," said Frank.

"And that's where the doll comes in," said Jonathan, putting the doll back together on the table. "I first learned this from the great advertising man David Ogilvy...."

"I suppose you knew him, too," said Jennifer, recalling her marketing class that studied Ogilvy at Wayne State.

"No, just through his books," said Jonathan.

Frank said, "You read all the time. Too much. Every day you eat here you are reading."

"This doll will show you something important," said Jonathan. "As you create your restaurant, you cannot hire people who are less, or smaller than you. If you do, and then they recommend people to work here that are less and smaller people than they are, look what happens. Juwan. A good person, maybe, but not a good prospect for the restaurant. Not if you're committed. Always hire people with the same size commitment that you have. Never a smaller-sized commitment to success. If you have that smaller person, keep interviewing, keep interviewing! Don't stop. "

Jonathan then began to take the doll apart again, this time opening each doll to smaller and smaller dolls on the table. He kept opening each doll and pulling out a smaller one...one doll after another doll, and it was incredible how many there were inside each other, doll after doll, until he got to this last tiny doll, as small as a thimble and holding it up between his fingers he said, "you will have a business full of mental midgets."

"He's right!" said Jennifer. "Vladek brought in Marianne who brought in her roommate Julie who recommended Juwan when you were hurting for help, Frank. Remember when Boris quit?"

"But Juwan is a good boy, as much as I hated him for a week," said Frank. "I met his uncle. Juwan has a good heart but he was on drugs. He is not a midget."

"You're right, Frank," said Jonathan. "Juwan is not a bad person. And if he gets himself into ongoing recovery, he could be a great person. Even a good employee. But you have to see that your job here is to *not* hire people smaller than you, commitment-wise. This has to be about commitment to a successful restaurant. You aren't a way-station for people who need jobs. You can't use your restaurant that way, because it confuses you about what you're up to here."

"I wish we could apply this lesson to customers," said Jennifer.

Jonathan jumped up from his seat.

"Thank you!" he shouted. "Thank you for saying that! Say it again!"

Jennifer looked started and said hesitantly, "I wish we could use this lesson for customers and not just employees."

"Wow," said Jonathan. "You just uncovered the master key to success right there, in that innocent wish. Because you *can*. You can create a team of customers, too, and almost nobody gets this. You can grow a customer base of people you want in here. People you choose. People who refer like-minded people. People who come in here over and over."

"Not just the softball teams and college kids," said Frank.

"They have their place, but you want a core list. Even a membership," said Jonathan. "At the very least, you want a mailing list of special guests."

Jonathan arranged all the dolls in order in a line on the table, from biggest to smallest.

"You want everyone you hire and everyone you serve to stand as tall as you do in their commitment to creating and enjoying a great restaurant experience and pleasing the customer," said Jonathan.

"I think I see," said Frank, picking up the smallest doll. "You think we have just hired too quickly. Without thinking who we want here."

"Exactly the point of the doll," said Jonathan as he put the *matryoshka* back together, doll by doll. "You hire too quickly, and you just serve whoever walks in. You use discounts, and that attracts the least desirable customers. You hire based on immediate needs, not long-term plans, and that attracts problem workers. Or, at best, simply uncommitted workers. Don't hire smaller. Ever."

"What about someone like Rosie?" Jennifer said, gesturing toward the waitress with red corn rows.

"Rosie's okay," said Jonathan. "But you want more than okay. You want someone special waiting on people. Someone your customers will really enjoy and get a kick out of. Someone who goes the extra mile. Every person here has the potential to affect the experience. We are selling an experience, not just a meal."

The waitress in red corn rows appeared over Jonathan's shoulder and set down his basted eggs, steamed spinach and smoked salmon. Frank looked down admiringly at the food and said, "Vladek. He is good. He is a good cook. He is not a small doll. He is a grandmother."

Jennifer smiled and looked over at Jonathan. Frank rested his hand on the Russian doll's head, looking like he had just caught a distant daydream of a far off land, and then he said, "May I be excused for a minute?" He slowly stood to leave the table. "I must check on some deliveries for tonight. I forgot about them."

Jonathan and Jennifer nodded as Frank left. Jennifer poured herself some water and said to Jonathan, "You eat, I'll talk." Jonathan nodded yes, his mouth full of the best basted eggs he had ever tasted.

"I noticed that you brought the newspaper ad in with you," said Jennifer. "Frank and the newspaper rep...Rhiannon I think her name is...made that ad and ran it forever."

"I thought the name was Mary Kay...."

"That's the radio rep," said Jennifer. "Anyway, we have no idea whether anyone ever saw the newspaper ad. Ever! But I want to tell you that one of the reasons I quit Wayne State is that I want to do this, and learn this. I took marketing classes, but I don't think they will give me what you can give me, and I don't want Frank doing the worrying about our marketing. So I've decided to do this part of the business, and Frank agrees. So your idea about creating a mailing list is exciting to me."

"That's great news," said Jonathan, between bites of salmon. "But Frank should know what you're doing. We should teach him everything. Everyone should know everything."

"Yes! I agree," said Jennifer. "But you are so successful, or at least it seems like you are, and everything you teach us is so powerful and simple and so impossible to forget...that I just want to learn how you've done it and how we can apply it."

"I am a failure," said Jonathan.

Jennifer said nothing.

"I have had four businesses fail, totally and completely, wiped out."

"You don't look old enough to have four total failures."

"That's how fast I went through them!" said Jonathan, with a smile.

"But your studio looks so successful, and your car, and your office in Detroit, and...."

"Yes, I am now successful, I will admit that," said Jonathan. "I even have more than one studio, and now other branches of business I'm involved in, all successful. But my failure is what taught me what I know. Without failing all those times, I would not have any certainty about this."

"Well, good," said Jennifer. "But does that mean we have to fail, too?"

"I think you're already there," said Jonathan with a twinkle in his eyes. "Or close enough. And no, people don't have to fail. But they do have to somehow get past all the myths that keep them in failure."

"Myths? Like what?"

"Like this ad," said Jonathan, reaching for the folded newspaper that said the Sunshine Inn had the best food and the best prices. "The reason you don't know whether this ad has brought anybody in is because it hasn't. It gives no real reason for people to come in. The little review at the bottom of the ad is good, but it's in small print and I doubt if anyone ever got to it."

"What about our promising best prices?" said Jennifer.

Jonathan pushed his finished plates to the side corner of the table so they could both get a clearer look at the ad. He poured himself a half cup of coffee and looked at Jennifer. She had just taken her notebook out and was finishing writing something down in response to what Jonathan had said. When she finished, Jonathan spoke again.

"What if you needed brain surgery?" said Jonathan.

"That's a pleasant breakfast-time thought," said Jennifer.

"And someone called you and said, 'I know where I can get you a really good price on brain surgery. I can get it done for you for next to nothing.' Would you be excited about that?"

"Of course not. I wouldn't touch that surgeon with a ten-foot pole."

"Well, believe it or not, that aversion you felt for something cheap is an aversion you will feel for anything cheap that you really value."

"Like a great dinner," said Jennifer.

"Like a great dining experience," said Jonathan.

"We have been lowering our prices and offering discount specials," said Jennifer.

"How has it worked?"

"More college students. Fraternity groups. Fairly rowdy. Not great for the atmosphere."

Jonathan said, "Okay, so they aren't ideal customers are they? The ones you attract with discounts never are. Let's talk about ideal customers. How many ideal customer types have come in because you lowered prices?"

"We haven't seen any."

Both Jonathan and Jennifer were silent for a while, letting the significance of how much money had been wasted on ineffective advertising sink in.

"Hold that thought," said Jonathan as he started to pack his things to leave. "Hold that insight, and I hope it is one. Tell me something, can Vladek do the after-lunch-hour kitchen work? Dinner prep, cooking, or whatever is done?"

"Yes, of course."

"Good, how about we make an appointment for tomorrow at two in the afternoon, you and Frank and me."

"Here?"

"No. We're going on a field trip. I want you to meet me at Boundaries, the big bookstore across town, on First Street and Birch Tree Road. We'll meet in their lobby area at two?"

"Sure, fine," said Jennifer. "But why a book store? Shouldn't we be looking at restaurants that do it right?"

"We're not going to look at how to do it right," said Jonathan. "We're going to look at the opposite of that. We're going to see a classic example of the wrong way to do business."

Chapter 12

Jonathan had arrived at the bookstore ten minutes early, and had the top down on his Ferrari, taking in the breezy summer afternoon while sitting in his open car with the CD player playing Chopin's Nocturne for Piano No. 8 in D flat major rather loudly. He was absent-mindedly leafing through a notebook when he felt a tap on his shoulder.

"Are you trying to impose your good taste in music on the rest of us?" said Jennifer.

Jonathan looked startled, then happy to see her. He turned off the music and got out of his car.

"You're early," he said, shaking her hand.

"Yes, and maybe it's good. I had a question for you."

Jonathan motioned to a wooden bench that sat between two birch trees and the two walked over and sat down.

"What's your question?" said Jonathan.

"Well, it's about your methods, or your strategy," Jennifer said. "It seemed like you were being all friendly to us and then when we had the robbery and Frank was at his lowest point ever was when you hit him the hardest. It was a little like hitting someone when they're down. I'm not arguing with the effect it had, because he really came around afterward, but why did you choose to do it that way?"

"People are the most teachable when they are in their worst trouble," said Jonathan.

"Really?" said Jennifer. "And that's because?"

"That's because they are the most awake at that time. They can really hear you."

"And when they're happy?"

"They're asleep."

Jennifer looked at Jonathan for a moment and smiled to herself. It seemed to her that everything this young man said was upside down...the opposite of her common sense view of life. But, yet, it had a ring of truth to it, a kind of purity she had never experienced, especially when the subject was business.

Jonathan said, "Frank was finally ready to listen."

"So you like trouble," said Jennifer.

"In a way, it can be the best thing, the best opportunity to grow. Problems always contain gifts. Whenever you have a problem, don't miss the gift inside...Hey, did you read the paper today?"

"Some of it."

"Did you read the obituaries by any chance?"

"No, I try not to."

"Oh, you should! They're actually about life, not death. Tributes to life! Anyway, Richard Eberhart, the prize-winning poet died yesterday. And I remembered hearing him read his poems once in a little lecture hall in Ann Arbor."

"My goodness. Classical music and poetry. Who are you trying to impress?"

"No, my point is this. He was 101 years old when he died. He was teaching and writing beautiful poems right up to the end. A full life! And in the obituary, do you know what he said made him a poet?"

"A commitment not to work for a living?"

"No, no. Please follow me here. What turned him into a poet was the fact that his mother died of cancer when he 18, and that same year his father lost his fortune and went broke."

"That would have turned most people into Juwan."

"That's my point! Right! Most people would have taken that tragedy and milked it for the rest of their lives. But you don't have to do that. That's what I was trying to do with you and Frank. Use the robbery as a turning point for the good, instead of letting it sink us lower and lower into depression and self-pity."

Jonathan stopped talking when he heard a distant sound. It was the distinctive rattling sound of Frank's truck as it pulled in to a parking spot near where they were sitting. Jonathan and Jennifer both looked up, smiled at the sound, and got up to greet him.

"I am late?" shouted Frank.

"No, you're not," said Jonathan. "We were early. Let's go inside."

"This is about the movie?" said Frank.

"Yes," said Jonathan. "I heard you liked that movie."

"This is Tom Hanks' store," said Frank, waving his beefy arm at the huge modern two-story Boundaries bookstore as they made their way into the lobby area.

"Exactly right!" said Jonathan. "Boy, you learn fast. This is just a little experiment I wanted to make, to show you something. I am here to buy a book, *Think and Grow Rich* by Napoleon Hill, and let's say I don't know where it is. Let's see what happens."

The three walked inside and surveyed the massive store. Frank pointed to a desk that said "Information" so all three of them waited in the line that was gathered at the information desk. There was a portly and heavily pierced young bookstore employee behind the Information desk who kept leaving his station behind the desk and then returning. The line didn't seem to be moving at all. After five minutes or more Jennifer spoke up.

"Let's try to use one of those computers they have around here."

"Good idea," said Jonathan.

"Not me," said Frank. "I would have to wait in line. I tried one of those once when I was looking for a cookbook and I couldn't get anything on it."

"They're easy," said Jennifer as they headed off to a computer standing between two aisles of books. When they got there Jennifer typed in "Napoleon Hill." The computer showed that there was one copy of the book in the Business section of the store and one copy in Self-Help. They went looking for Business and saw from a sign that it was upstairs.

"Where's Self-Help?" asked Jonathan.

"Upstairs, too," said Jennifer pointing at the sign that had all the departments and their locations.

All three climbed the stairs and found themselves in the children's section with no Business or Self-Help in sight. Finally they found Business at the far north corner of the upper level. Frank looked on the shelves.

"Hill?" he said.

"Yes, Napoleon Hill," said Jonathan. "*Think and Grow Rich.*"

"Maybe buy two copies so we have one, too?" said Frank with a laugh. "I would like to grow rich just by thinking about it!"

"Hill, Hill, Hill," said Jennifer running her fingers down the books. "There's none here."

"Okay," said Jonathan. "Let's try Self-Help."

After a long fruitless search in Self-Help, Jennifer called out "Wait! Here it is!"

"Where was it?" said Jonathan.

"It was misfiled, out of alphabetic order, it was in the J's, it just caught my eye," said Jennifer.

"Okay," said Jonathan, "Let's go buy it."

When they got back downstairs they saw a very long line behind the counter that had six registers. Only two registers were operational, even though there were five people behind the counter. There were three GO TO NEXT REGISTER signs in front of people. The music in the store was inordinately loud, some kind of jazz fusion piece with dueling trumpets overloading the speaker system in a way that entered the head through the temple more than the ear.

"This will take forever," said Frank.

"Why don't you just buy it over the internet," said Jennifer.

"Because I want you to experience this," said Jonathan. "This is about your restaurant. This is about lack of respect. I have come in here a few times, but they don't know me here. They have never known me here, and they will never know me here. They don't want to know me."

After a seemingly endless wait in line a young woman yelled out "Next!" in a voice that sounded like a mixture of disgust and irritation.

"Wow," said Jennifer. "It feels like we're in the Motor Vehicle Department."

"Exactly," said Jonathan.

As Jonathan stepped up to make his purchase, Frank and Jennifer stood behind him, listening to what he said to the young woman.

"Are you having a busy day?" said Jonathan.

"It's been awful," she said without making eye contact.

"Why is it awful?"

"We've been slammed since morning. But I'm like, who cares now? I get off in fifteen minutes. Finally. You know what I mean? Do you want our discount card?"

"No."

"Here's your change."

"Thank you for serving me," said Jonathan.

The young woman said nothing. Even before the three were leaving the counter they heard her yelling, "Next!" and this time her voice sounded even nastier.

"That was not a great experience," said Jennifer, as all three gathered outside the store.

"We are not like that at the restaurant," said Frank. "We treat people nice."

"You do," said Jonathan "What people you have. And once they are there. But there's so much more you can do. For example, I don't think you really know your customers, Frank. Do you know any of their names?"

"I don't get it," said Frank.

"Can we all fit in your truck?" said Jonathan.

"Yes," said Jennifer. "It will be a squeeze, but we can."

"Then I'm going to buy you that second copy of *Think and Grow Rich*," said Jonathan.

Soon all three were squeezed into Frank's brown Dodge pickup hurtling down Woodward Avenue listening to "The Polish Hour" on Frank's radio, featuring robust trios singing behind accordion music.

"Dad, what are we listening to?" said Jennifer.

"It's fine!" said Jonathan. "I love it!"

"Tell me how we are like that bookstore," said Frank, searching for the road Jonathan said to turn off at. Finally he saw it and they made a left turn into Birmingham where Jonathan directed him to a row of small shops with parking meters on the street.

"Park right here and I'll tell you in a few minutes," said Jonathan. "First, let's go in here."

The Maroon Unicorn was a bookstore that looked like a Swiss cottage on the outside, but once they got inside they could see that it stretched back a long way with an enormous high ceiling with books on shelves stacked to the top and ladders on wheels. There was also a descending staircase to a basement filled with books.

"Wow," said Jennifer. "This is bigger than it looks."

As soon as they entered an old man behind the front counter smiled and said, "Welcome, people! Is this your first time here?"

"Yes," said Frank, and before he could say anything else the old man looked at Jonathan and said, "I remember you, young man. You've been here. You bought the Father Brown mysteries by Chesterton."

"Yes!" said Jonathan. "Good memory. But my friends are new."

"Wonderful," said the old man. "Let me know if I can help you in any way. Fiction is upstairs, nonfiction is down. We keep it simple."

All three went downstairs to look for Napoleon Hill as a barely audible but relaxing classical piano piece played in the background, giving the bookstore a quiet, timeless old English feeling.

As they reached the bottom of the stairs a short, stout old woman looked up and said, "Mr. Berkley! How good to see you again."

"Hello, Anna," said Jonathan. "This is Frank, and this is Jennifer and we're looking for Napoleon Hill, *Think and Grow Rich*."

"Right over here," Anna said and she led them down the aisle and found the book on the shelf and pulled it down. She smiled again at Jonathan as she handed him the book. "How do you like your Father Brown mysteries?"

"They are every bit as good as I remembered them," said Jonathan.

"Have you read *The Man Who Was Thursday*?" said Anna.

"No," said Jonathan.

"That's another Chesterton mystery, but it doesn't have Father Brown in it. I bet you'd love it. We don't have it but I can order it for you. No charge for ordering it, you can come in and look at it and see if you'd like it."

"That would be great," said Jonathan.

"I'll send you a postcard when it's in," said Anna.

"Do you want me to give you my address?"

"No, it's in our system," said Anna.

The three bookstore visitors proceeded up the stairs and went to the front counter where the old man smiled at them again.

"Find everything you need?" he said.

"Yes!" said Frank. "Thank you."

The old man handed Frank and Jennifer each a little packet of papers, cards and a folder.

"You may take these home," he said. "There are coupons for your next visit in, and fifty percent off the next three books you buy here when you sign up for our newsletter. You can get the newsletter by email or in the mail, your choice."

"Thank you," said Frank.

"And because you're new to us," said the old man, "Here are two gift certificates to the Starbucks next door, so next time you come—or, when you leave today, you can stop there for a refreshment."

"Wow," said Jennifer. "Thank you."

Jonathan finished paying and all three walked into the afternoon sun and breeze of Birmingham. They could smell the pansies and lilacs from the park across the street, and all three gave each other that look that says we have just had a rather pleasant experience together.

"They remember you," said Frank. "When was the last time you were here?"

"A year ago," said Jonathan.

"They must have some system," said Jennifer.

"They do," said Jonathan.

"What do you think their system is?" said Frank.

"They care," said Jonathan.

"We care, too," said Frank.

"You care about your cooking," said Jonathan. "And you care about your troubles. They care about me."

"Who are you to them?" said Jennifer. "Do they know you from somewhere else?"

"I am their customer!" said Jonathan. "That's enough for them. From the minute I first walked in, they wanted to know all about me. And I know you guys are nice and friendly to people who eat in your restaurant, but that's not enough. We need to increase the customer's importance to you. We need to know about the people who come in, how they heard about us, what they like about us, because that's how we'll get more people like them."

"So you took us here to show us how well they know you," said Frank.

"Yes," said Jonathan. "And between now and two weeks from now they will do some other little thing, some little unexpected touch, to please me."

"Can we learn this too?" said Frank.

"Of course! Absolutely! You are the perfect people for this kind of approach," said Jonathan. "We will grow your restaurant using this principle. It's an old military principle, by the way. The most impactful military principle ever known."

"What military principle is it?" said Frank.

"The element of surprise."

Chapter 13

Juwan Jefferson was sitting in a circle of chairs in the main dining hall at the Chesney Brothers Recovery Center in upstate Michigan. Dinner had ended two hours ago, and as the other drug and alcohol recovery patients came in to take their seats in the circle, Juwan thought back to his visit this morning from his Uncle Luther.

They had been sitting at a table on the patio overlooking the lake, and Uncle Luther was telling Juwan about the sequence of events that got him here.

"So how can you afford this place, tell me again, Uncle Lou," said Juwan.

"Your boss would not press charges," said Luther. "And your boss's partner knew the D.A. and talked to him about getting you here."

"My boss's partner?" said Juwan. "My boss doesn't have a partner. It's just him."

"Frank does have a partner," said Luther, pulling a manila folder up from below his chair, "and his name is here somewhere because he signed the contract and made the payment. Here it is: Berkley. Jonathan Berkley."

"I have no idea who that is," said Juwan. "Why would they do this?"

"Because Frank believed me," said Luther. "I told him you were getting ready to take the safe back when the police came. I told him the reason the money was still there was because you and I decided to return it."

"I was going to kick this on my own," said Juwan. "This place is nice and all that, and the people and the nurses are nice, but I feel funny being here. How will I ever pay anyone back?"

"Frank says payback will be getting your life straight," said Luther.

"I feel bad because Frank's restaurant is really hurting right now," said Juwan. "I was mopping the floor that morning, my second day without using, and I just started to panic. I started throwing up, and I saw all these people at the window, and I knew they weren't real, they were like from my games, from X-Men and Wolverine, but I was even more scared because they weren't real…I knew I had to score just to do something to take the fear away."

"What changed your mind?" said Luther. "When I found you, you were just staring at the safe."

"I found your Southern Comfort, Uncle Lou, and that was enough to make the fear go away."

"I thought you smelled bad!" Luther laughed. "But, Juwan, that stuff is nasty, too. That's how you lost your mother. To liquor. I never should have saved that bottle."

"I know, I know," said Juwan. "I'm learning that here. Alcohol is a drug, too, if you use it like I do."

Luther looked at his nephew for a long time as neither of them spoke. The ducks on the water were silently floating across the lake, and the breezes rippled the willow branches as Juwan shifted his chair.

"Whoever this partner is," said Juwan, "I owe him. And Frank needs him. Frank needs a partner because he's a great cook, but he's kind of clueless about the rest. I really let them down."

"Juwan, you can recover. You can have a life. That would be the best thing you could do for Frank right now, you could give him the good news that you have used this place to recover."

"You didn't need a place like this," said Juwan. "I remember you got straight on your own."

"I would have loved it!" said Luther. "But I had my meetings in the church basement, and they were enough for me. People recover, Juwan."

"I hope I can."

"Just do it all. Do all the work. If they have steps to work, work the steps. This is your new life. Do this well. You are a good boy. My sister always told me how much you helped her. You can help a lot of people, Juwan. That's how this works. Once you get your recovery, you do what they call 'Twelve Step work' and you help others. You've got to give it away to keep it. There are a lot of young men like you who would listen to you, Juwan. They wouldn't listen to me, but they would listen to you."

Juwan was listening carefully. Luther went on.

"No more self-pity, Juwan. You need to work. Go to work on yourself here. Throw yourself into this, like you used to play basketball. What did your coach always say?"

"Make each day your masterpiece."

"Right! Make each day your masterpiece! Do this recovery that way, too. One day at a time. Give it all you've got, one day at a time."

Luther slowly got up to go. He pulled out an envelope from his folder.

"What's that?"

"It's a card for you from the people at the restaurant."

"Jennifer and Vladek know I'm here?"

"Everybody knows everything, Juwan, now make them proud."

Juwan's eyes filled as he hugged his Uncle Luther goodbye.

Chapter 14

Jennifer had seen the red Ferrari pull up to the restaurant parking lot five minutes ago and still Jonathan had not come in. He was probably listening to Chopin finish his piano concerto, she thought, shaking her head and going back to filling in the accounting ledger. Finally, she could stand it no longer so she got up and walked outside to the car.

The top was down, as usual, and Jonathan was sitting in the car, putting a CD away, just as she had suspected when she walked up to him saying, "Just can't get enough of that classical music?"

"Oh, hi, Jennifer, no," said Jonathan. "Listen, do you have a minute? Listen to this. This is amazing. You need to hear this."

Jonathan fumbled to find the CD he had just taken out of the player in the dash. Jennifer shook her head and smiled, "No! We have work to do. I know you only have a half hour today, I need every minute. I can't listen to music, now."

"It's not music," said Jonathan. "*Listen* to this!"

Jonathan put the CD in and pushed the play button and adjusted the volume up so Jennifer could hear it from where she stood outside the car by his window. A low, gravelly voice started to speak from the speakers, "Hello, Mr. Berkley, this is Charlie your mechanic and I wanted you to know that everything looked fine today on your 308. Marcus did the tune up and the oil and changed your air filter and gave you a new fan belt because yours didn't look so good, but that knock you heard was gone after we did the oil change so you should be fine. Any trouble, just call us, and also look in your glove compartment. There's a gift certificate to Sweet

Tomatoes in there for you, so have a lunch on us someday. We appreciate your business."

Jonathan pushed the button that ejected the CD and put it into his folder and got out of the car and put the top back up.

Jennifer said, "Wow! That was your mechanic?"

"Yes," said Jonathan. "Isn't that great?"

"How can he afford to do that?" said Jennifer. "I mean, the time it must take to make that CD, to begin with, and then the certificate to Sweet Tomatoes, how much is that?"

"That's ten dollars," said Jonathan, "And it probably took him three minutes to make the CD."

"Do you think it's worth it?"

"Look, I spent over three thousand dollars with them last year on the Ferrari. I have referred at least four other people to them. I love them because of the extra touches they do. The guy at the cash register tells me what work was done, but to hear it from Charlie himself while I'm driving away, that's just a magical touch for me."

Jonathan and Jennifer walked into the restaurant together and moved through the empty tables to the back table where Jennifer had her work spread out.

"Is Frank joining us?" said Jonathan.

"He's visiting one of our suppliers. We are way behind on payments to them and Frank said he was going over there in person to do some begging, as he put it. I have to tell you, things are not looking good right now. We all have good intentions, but we may be too late to really do this."

"Jennifer," said Jonathan, "I know how you feel right now. It feels like everyone's against you. Everyone's mad at you...."

"The IRS person called here yesterday. We've been assigned an agent! I feel like a criminal."

"I understand. But you have to get one big truth into your head: Everyone is on your side."

"It doesn't feel that way."

"I know it doesn't feel that way, but we have to set feelings aside here and deal with truth and reality. Emotion won't serve us right now."

"Okay," said Jennifer. "I'll take the bait. How is everyone on our side?"

"No one wins if you fail," said Jonathan. "Not Frank's suppliers, not even the IRS. The only way they win, in the end, is if you win. So get that. They all want you to win. They're just not acting like it in your eyes. But it's our leverage with them. We will sell our success to them as being in their best interest as well as ours."

Jennifer said, "We just need some money right now."

"Okay, I hear you," said Jonathan as they both sat down at her table. "Let's begin by having more people come in to the restaurant. That's where the money comes from."

"You know we're out of advertising money," said Jennifer.

"Well, that's okay because it never brought people in anyway."

"We don't think."

"If you don't know, it didn't," said Jonathan.

"I read a study at Wayne State," said Jennifer, "and it said that people...consumers...have comfort zones. And they have places they are comfortable patronizing. Places they trust."

"Right, true," said Jonathan. "Because if someone is going to bring a guest or a business partner to lunch here, they will want to have tried it and liked it."

"So the trick would be to get them in here once, so they know about us," said Jennifer.

"Not just know about us."

"Whatever."

"They have to have *experienced* us," said Jonathan. "That's the big fallacy we want to avoid, the fallacy that says it's important that they *know about* us. We need to ignore that. What's important is that they experience us. That they have actually been in here! If they've been here once, the odds are good that they will come again."

"So how do we get them in here the first time?"

"We make them an offer they can't refuse."

"Okay," said Jennifer. "Are you a *Godfather* fan?"

Jonathan started to say yes but then stopped and said, "What did you just say?"

"I was just asking you if you liked *The Godfather*, because you used that line from the movie, making them an offer they can't refuse."

"Our grand opening could be Godfather Days at the Sunshine Inn!" said Jonathan, smacking his hand on the table. "We could get the word to every business and resident within a two mile radius of the restaurant, and there are a ton of them, that we are going to have Godfather Days at the Sunshine Inn, 'An offer you can't refuse: Bring a friend to lunch and your friend gets their main dish free!'"

Jennifer smiled and then let the smile start to fade. "We can't afford that," she said. "Giving a main dish away for free? And how would we get the word out?"

Jonathan pushed his chair part way back from the table. It was almost noon and the restaurant was almost completely empty. Two men in business suits were sitting in the front corner, but the rest of the tables were empty.

"Look around you, Jennifer," said Jonathan as he gestured toward all the empty tables. "This is what you can't afford. This empty restaurant."

Jennifer looked around and nodded. The lack of people was something she had become accustomed to. To see this place full would be almost disorienting. But she would love it.

Chapter 15

Wayne State was a true city campus, with buildings in downtown Detroit that looked like government bureaucracy buildings rather than the ivy-covered picture Jennifer always held of college life.

But her desire was to learn business and marketing, so the school had suited her just fine, and as she walked the long grey concrete walk to Tidwell Hall to see her professor, Dr. Orville Bly, she felt sad, on the one hand, but also quite satisfied. Sad that this was the last signature she needed to officially drop out of school, but satisfied that this process would be over and she could devote her full attention to saving the restaurant.

"Dr. Bly will see you now," said the young lady at the reception desk without looking up, and Jennifer walked in to his office and let the door close behind her.

"Jennifer Mills!" said Dr. Bly as he looked up at her over his reading glasses and motioned to a chair in front of his desk. He was a heavy, sixty-something man with a bushy beard who looked like he was trying to look even older. None of his clothes matched, with a striped maroon shirt, a fluorescent green tie and dirty taupe suspenders holding him together. His desk was piled high with books and papers and three of the four walls in his office were jammed ceiling-high with books.

"Please don't tell me this is true," said Dr. Bly, pointing to the drop forms Jennifer held in her hand.

"Yes, sir, I'm afraid I'm leaving Wayne," said Jennifer. "And I want to thank you for agreeing to sign this."

"Miss Mills, I am usually happy to sign these, but in your case I'm not. You are one of my best students! Your last paper was one of the best explanations of Dr. Eli Goldratt's work I've ever had submitted to me."

"Thank you, sir."

"Why on earth are you doing this?"

"I'm going to help my father with his business."

"May I ask what kind of business it is?"

"It's a restaurant, sir, in Royal Oak."

Dr. Bly frowned, then sighed, then slowly turned his high-backed swivel chair so that he could look out over the top of his glasses that were riding low on his nose. He appeared to be looking out his window at the parking garage across the alley. He was shaking his head slowly.

"I take it you disapprove, sir."

"Miss Mills, Miss Mills."

"But I am looking forward to some real-world business experience, and we have a person who is advising us who has had tremendous success in other fields."

"Miss Mills, I will sign your forms but not until I have a chance to make a counterpoint of sorts," said Dr. Bly.

Jennifer had dreaded this moment. All of her other professors and teachers signed her forms and wished her well without any argument. But she knew Dr. Bly and his opinion of business ventures, which, for a professor in the Business School, was extremely negative.

"Business is a good thing to study, but very often a bad thing to get into," said Dr. Bly. "I had hoped you would follow your fine academic work into graduate school somewhere and go on to teach. Your papers are so good, and your thinking, while a little on the conservative side for my taste, has been crystal clear and always backed up with thorough research. This is a major disappointment right here, that I am signing these forms."

"But, Dr. Bly," said Jennifer. "How can business be a good thing to study but a bad thing to get into? What could be a better education than running your own business?"

Dr. Bly allowed himself a laugh and then a long, lingering smile. It was the kind of smile that told Jennifer that he thought he knew a great deal more than most other people on this subject.

Dr. Bly said, "One can study sharks, Miss Mills, without swimming out in the ocean to join them. Once can study the virus that causes AIDS without trying to contract the disease."

"I hardly think our family restaurant can be compared to a disease," said Jennifer.

"And you are so young," said Dr. Bly, "that you can think that. But once you have lived awhile as I have, you will become a little sadder about these matters, but wiser."

"I plan not to," said Jennifer.

"Not to what?"

"Get sadder as I grow older. I've seen it happen, and I don't plan on it myself."

Dr. Bly allowed himself a bemused smile and finally said, "Miss Mills, business is based on greed. You know that, I know that...."

"Business is a service, sir, inside a free enterprise system, wherein the emphasis is on 'free,' and I intend to participate in it freely. You are free, too, to use or not use any business you like."

Dr. Bly gestured at his Starbucks cup on the cluttered desk and took a sip from it before holding it up to Jennifer.

"Look at this!" said Dr. Bly. "Do you know what this one cup cost? Can you tell me that when a business charges as much as Starbucks does for a cup of coffee that it is anything but a form of greed?"

Jennifer was ready to leave. She looked at the unsigned drop forms and reluctantly made a mental note to stay a maximum of three more minutes before insisting on leaving.

Jennifer said, "I'm sure you must have free coffee available to you in this building, Dr. Bly."

"Have you ever had it?" he said with a roaring laugh.

"Well, then that just might be the service that Starbucks is giving you. Really delicious, satisfying coffee instead of the machine-made coffee in this building. Plus the fun of being in there, and how cool it is to have a Starbucks cup in your hand while you talk to people. All those things are worth something to you, or you would not have bought your coffee there."

"I admire your fierce naiveté," said Dr. Bly, smiling again. "But I also fear for you. You are just the kind of lamb that business enjoys slaughtering."

"I am a woman, Dr. Bly, not a lamb, and I will succeed at what I am about to do. I will not be slaughtered, and I will count your course as one of the good experiences in my life, one of the strengthening factors in my thinking, and I will always be grateful to you for your teaching even if I don't share your view of business. May I please have my forms signed?"

Dr. Bly raised his eyebrows a little while trying to separate the compliment from the argument in what Jennifer had just said. He found the forms on his desk, pushed his glasses into place with one finger, and slowly signed all three, one after the other, as if he was signing death warrants.

"I hope to see you back," he said, "and I hope the experience will not sour you on life so much that you don't want to come back."

Once her forms were safely in hand, Jennifer stood to leave and said, "That's *your* life view you're talking about, sir, not mine. I have a wish for you, too. That sometime in the next year you come into our restaurant, the Sunshine Inn in Royal Oak, so that you can see real life happening. Real service. Real success. There will be nothing theoretical about that experience."

Dr. Bly turned away from her as she was leaving and Jennifer felt strangely stronger and clearer as she walked out of his office and down the hall of the Tidwell Building toward the business life that was awaiting her. She had no idea that her biggest problem yet would be barely an hour away.

Chapter 16

Jennifer's car pulled up to the back of the Sunshine Inn and before she had even turned the engine off, Vladek, Frank's kitchen assistant, was at her car window looking terrified.

"My goodness, Vladek," said Jennifer. "Couldn't I come inside first?"

Vladek said, "It's Frank."

Jennifer gathered her school notebooks and purse and stepped out of the car holding Vladek's gaze with her own.

"And?" she said impatiently.

"Frank is at the airport, and he is going back home! All the way! To Europe, to the old country! He is finished. He called an hour ago. I didn't know how to reach you at the school."

"Finished?"

"He said our suppliers were suing us and we would have to close the restaurant and he left you a letter."

"Our suppliers are suing us?" said Jennifer. "All of them? That's impossible. So, what happened? Which supplier got to him?"

Jennifer and Vladek walked through the back half of the kitchen out into Frank's darkened little office.

Jennifer said, "When does his plane leave? Where did he say the letter was? What do I...."

"The letter is in the big refrigerator, I found it earlier, and I left it there, by the onions."

"Can you bring it to me?" Jennifer said.

"Yes, and the plane leaves at six o'clock for London."

Jennifer looked at the wooden cuckoo clock on the wall next to Frank's poster from the musical *Hair*! It would be two hours 'til flight time.

"What have we done about the restaurant?" Jennifer asked.

"Closed," said Vladek. "I sent everyone home. I put up a sign. I said it was temporary."

"We've got to page him," said Jennifer, almost as if to herself. She took out her cell phone and opened it. Then she stopped to think. In her purse she found a business card and handed it to Vladek.

"Will you call this man?" she said. "This is Jonathan. You know him, the one who...."

"Oh, our helping friend with the *Magnum* car?"

"Yes, see if you can ask him to come here or at least call here right away, and tell him what's happening while I call the airport to see if I can page Frank."

Vladek hurried to the wall phone in the kitchen and began punching in Jonathan's number while Jennifer called information. This wasn't going to be easy, she thought. Her father had always said that if it got bad enough someday he would just disappear. She wondered what had set him off. Who had he been to see that threatened to sue him?

"He's coming right over!" Vladek said. "Mr. Jonathan. He is on his way, he said."

Jennifer smiled and waved him away as she finally got someone on the line at the airport, "Can you page Mr. Frank Mills? The message? Tell him to call his daughter at the business, she has a family emergency, he must call before he gets on the flight. He is flying to London in two hours or less, whatever that flight is. Okay. Okay, thank you. It's 313-677-5566. Thank you."

Jennifer sat back in Frank's big chair and stared at Vladek. He shrugged his shoulders and she motioned for him to take a seat.

"Now. Who threatened to sue us?" she said to Vladek.

"Wheat and Bread Center is what Frank said," said Vladek. "I told him we could use another company and he said it was too late."

"He doesn't understand," said Jennifer. "In his old country, people were put in jail for nothing. Here, any mention of anything like that, or anything legal, and he panics. This whole situation isn't good for him. I don't know what to do, but I hate to see him just panic and run."

"He is going there to die," said Vladek.

"Nonsense," said Jennifer.

"No, he told me many times. When he wants to die, he will go to the old country. He even knows where he wants people to find him."

"Okay, I need a minute," said Jennifer.

Vladek nodded and left her alone. Jennifer sat in silence with her eyes closed for almost 20 minutes. All she could hear was the sound of Vladek cleaning the dining area.

There was a noise that woke her from her meditative state. The rumble of the engine of Jonathan's car could be heard outside the back door. Jennifer noticed that it was strange to hear his car back there, but he must have seen that the restaurant was closed and knew they'd be in the back.

"I told him to come in back," said Vladek, poking his head in. They both listened to the outside engine rumble again before shutting down.

Vladek whispered, "That is some kind of beautiful red car."

Jennifer jumped up to open the back door and let Jonathan in. She briefed Jonathan on the situation and poured him an iced tea as he moved over to sit on a tall stool.

"Will you talk to him when he calls back from the airport?" Jennifer said.

"Yes, but let's have something good we can tell him," said Jonathan. "Let's have some kind of news to be able to give Frank when he calls because I don't think just plain persuading...or pleading, is going to work this time."

Jennifer pulled up a stool and opened a can of fruit juice for herself.

"What news?"

"News about the creditor and the restaurant."

"There is no news, though."

"We will make some news. Can you get me the owner of the bakery or bread supply place Frank was at today? Can you get him on the phone for me?"

Jennifer hopped off her stool to get Frank's address book and came back shaking her head.

"He's not a great guy to talk to," she said. "His name is Ralph Mallis and I've dealt with him before. A real psycho. Minor league mafia type."

Jonathan was already dialing the number.

"Mr. Mallis, this is Jonathan Berkley calling you from Frank Mills' office at the Sunshine Inn, and I represent Mr. Mills for today, sir, and would like to see if I can solve your current credit problem with this business."

Jonathan listened for a while and then held his phone away from his ear as an enraged little voice crackled in the air. Jonathan was smiling, and Jennifer and Vladek didn't know whether to laugh or not.

"Mr. Mallis, how much cash would you like delivered to your place of business today?" Jonathan asked. Jonathan then waited for a while and then jotted some numbers down before saying, "Sir, that will be no problem. I will bring that amount by myself. Now let me ask you another question. If I were to double that amount, would you be willing to do me the favor of calling Mr. Mills' message line and leaving him a real and heartfelt apology? You can use the extra money to keep us supplied in good standing for a few months."

Jonathan held the phone back from his ear again as Vladek and Jennifer both grinned.

"Well, then I'll just bring the first amount then," said Jonathan. "No? Oh, really? You'd consider it? No, sir. No, sir. It is not unfair to require an apology because you know Frank Mills, and you knew what threatening him with a lawsuit would do to him, and I know that you have other customers who are also behind in payments to you and you don't treat them that way. Or maybe you do. But I also know that you might want to continue to do business with someone who can easily pay you twice the number you mentioned in cash, so I know your apology will be a good one. I'll have Vladek…you know Vladek? Yes, that's Vladek. I'll have Vladek bring the payment over immediately and I expect your apology on Frank's message line. Yes. Thank you."

Jonathan pulled out his checkbook and wrote a check for Vladek.

"Vladek, take this to the Northern Trust Bank, just a few blocks down from here on Woodward Avenue, cash it, and get it over to

Mr. Mallis right away. Show him the money and make sure he calls before you leave. Make sure you hear him apologize. Big time."

"Yes, sir," Vladek said.

"Then get back here fast."

"You want me back?" said Vladek, looking at Jennifer.

Jonathan said, "Yes! We've got work to do! You and I are going to open this restaurant and start cooking!"

Jennifer frowned and looked doubtful.

Jonathan said, "How soon can we get everyone back in to work?"

"They all live nearby," said Jennifer. "We could probably get them back right away."

"Good!" said Jonathan.

Jennifer looked upset.

Jonathan said, "What's bothering you, Jennifer? What's the trouble?"

"Well," said Jennifer. "This doesn't feel right. We are using your money now? Where's the lesson in that? I thought you said we could work and think our way out of this, and now you just write a big check."

"The check isn't to save your business," said Jonathan. "I don't care about Ralph Mallis. He can go hang. We could use a new supplier and pay Mallis later. The check is to save Frank. It's a symbolic gesture. It's not the money, it's the gesture."

"It feels like it just puts us in more debt."

"It does not. In fact, I'll have that money back in a matter of days if we all pull together on this."

"Really!"

Jonathan got up from his stool and put his hand on Jennifer's arm and said to her, "When Frank calls, I want him to know two things. One: the Ralph Mallis problem has been solved and Mallis has left him an apology. And, two: this restaurant is open and will stay open and will succeed with or without Frank Mills and he can go back to the old country to die or he can help us make his dream come true. His choice."

Chapter 17

Frank had debated long and hard about whether to even respond to the page in the airport. On the one hand, he had a feeling it was a last-ditch attempt to talk him out of leaving. On the other hand, it might be some kind of family emergency. What if it was? What if Jennifer was hurt?

He wrestled with that scenario awhile. Why did he tell Vladek about his decision to leave? And how is it that he didn't mind going back to the old country to disappear and kill himself in the woods by the old farmland, but he couldn't stand not being there for Jennifer if she were hurt? How could both be true? How did the shame of being sued by that Ralph Mallis man push him over the edge?

"I just couldn't picture myself in court," Frank whispered to himself as he got up to look for the courtesy phone to see what the page was about. "Standing in front of a judge, admitting to my failures. The shame is too much. Better that everything collapse, I go away, and Jennifer can start a new life. She'll get over it. She'll learn the lesson, even. Don't start a business. Work for someone who knows how."

Frank stared at the courtesy phone before taking the white receiver off the wall. He had an hour and a half before the plane was to leave for its first stop in London. The Detroit airport was alive and buzzing with activity. It seemed to him that everyone had a cell phone and someone very important to talk to. Frank found himself wishing he had a cell phone and someone important to talk to about this whole idea of quitting and leaving. But who could

Frank talk to? Jennifer would just tell him she believed in him and this Jonathan man would help us fix everything. Jonathan had been so kind, it was true. But Frank thought Frank was the problem, and nothing could change the fact that Frank was Frank. A good cook? Certainly. But a worthy man? No longer. He was being sued.

Frank finally took the phone off the hook and listened to his airport message. He put the phone down and slowly walked to a pay phone to call the restaurant number as the message requested. He was surprised when Jonathan answered the phone.

"Sunshine Inn!" Jonathan said.

Frank paused, not knowing what to say. He thought they would close the restaurant. Finally Frank spoke softly, "There is a family emergency? This is Frank."

"Yes, there is a family emergency, and you are it," said Jonathan. "You have a restaurant here with no master chef. You have customers that Vladek and I are cooking for. That's an emergency, and Jennifer is trying to solve it, and she is your family, and for now, so am I, Frank, so please get on back so we can get back on track."

"It's too late," said Frank. "You don't understand, kind sir, kind young man. I have suffered great shame now and I must not continue."

"Frank, I do understand. I understand debts. I myself have had business failures, and gone broke. Four out of five businesses go under, Frank! And I spoke to Mr. Mallis at your main bakery. I know exactly what he said to you."

Frank said nothing.

Jonathan said, "Come home, Frank. We need you. Mr. Mallis has already apologized to you. He's left you a message. When we hang up, you can call back here and listen to it."

"You have helped me with him?"

"Frank, you are not alone in this. You think you should be able to do this alone, but that is not strength, Frank, that is weakness. Getting help is strength."

"How is that strength?"

"Because it means you care more about a result than you do about looking good. Getting help means you care more about reaching a goal than you do about your own pride. You care more about succeeding than you do about how strong you appear to be. Getting help is strength. Going it alone is weakness."

Frank said nothing.

"Frank, you have a picture of DiMaggio right here on your office wall."

"A hero, not like me," said Frank.

"You're right! He's not like you because he got help. Every day. From coaches and trainers and hitting instructors, he got help. He got coached. He looked at film of his swing, and he let people tell him what to change, and what to fix. He cared more about a great result than he did about going it alone. Going it alone is weak, Frank. It's small. You need to be a bigger man than you have been. You don't need to get smaller. Running away makes you smaller. When someone walks away from you they get smaller and smaller the farther they walk and finally you can't even see them any more."

"I don't believe there is an apology," said Frank.

"Call back and listen to it. I am hanging up. We will be expecting you, but if you don't return, don't expect us to cry for you. You will have caused us a great burden and you will have to take a much deeper shame to your grave. Because you will have left us when we needed you most."

Jonathan hung up the phone, turned around and saw Jennifer staring at him.

Jennifer said, "Are you sure you're doing the right thing? Don't you think I should talk to him, or do something a little less brutal?"

"Frank's a proud man who doesn't feel much like a man. I wanted to reach him there, and touch that part...."

"...the DiMaggio part...."

"Yes."

Jennifer walked in a slow circle and picked up Frank's favorite mixing spoon and smacked it on the counter shouting, "I hate him for this!"

Jonathan saw that she was starting to cry. He put his arm around her shoulder and let a long minute elapse while she cried before he said to her, "I know. But it will be all right."

As the next hour unfolded Vladek and Jonathan worked the kitchen while Jennifer waited on tables. Fortunately for them, the

Sunshine Inn wasn't very busy and the orders were easy to fill. Jennifer was torn between fear and sadness about her father and the laughter she couldn't hold back whenever she came into the kitchen and saw Jonathan stirring a pot or looking anxiously into the oven.

As she walked into the kitchen both Jonathan and Vladek looked up expectantly, worried that this time the order would be too challenging. Jennifer smiled and sat on a stool.

"All clear," she said. "The last table just left. Julie's cleaning up. There shouldn't be anyone else tonight. Fortunately it's Sunday. Early closing."

With a sigh of relief Jonathan sat down next to her as Vladek began carrying pots to the sink.

"What do we do now?" Jennifer said to Jonathan, knowing that he couldn't possibly have an answer to that question. Jonathan opened his mouth to speak and before he could say anything, they both turned their heads toward the noise at back door and the distinct rattling sound they had both come to know so well.

It was the sound of Frank's truck.

Chapter 18

Jonathan and Jennifer didn't waste any time talking to Frank about why he left or why he came back, they just wanted to show him how *needed* he was for the business to work, so their embraces had a happy urgency to them.

Jonathan went into the dining area and slid two tables together and put yellow legal pads out for Frank and Jennifer.

"What are we doing?" asked Frank.

"We are reinventing this business, Frank," said Jonathan. "So tell the employees to go home. We'll clean up, ourselves. We need privacy, because tonight it's just the three of us, until the sun comes up tomorrow if need be, but we're going to start this business all over again."

Frank went back into the kitchen to talk to Vladek, and Jennifer smiled across the table at Jonathan.

"Go easy on him," she said.

"No," said Jonathan. "Now's the time to go hard. He's ready. We can't go soft right now. We have to change the very nature of our approach to marketing this place."

Jonathan pulled an old newspaper section from his briefcase and spread it out on the table. Frank came in and took a seat. Vladek followed shortly behind him with a pitcher of iced tea and three glasses.

"Thank you, Vladek," said Jonathan. "See you tomorrow… right, Frank?"

"Right," said Frank, looking at Vladek, and holding out his hand to him. "And thank you, my friend."

Vladek stared at the three of them with all the pads and papers spread across the table. He broke into a big smile and turned and left.

Jennifer watched Vladek close and lock the front door of the restaurant and then turned to her father and said, "You know, Dad, I left school for this. For what we are doing right now. And I am here one hundred percent for this being my whole life right now. Life starts tonight."

"I wish you hadn't done that," Frank said. "I always wanted school for you."

Jonathan said, "Maybe you'll be glad she did leave school for now, Frank, because life wasn't working for either of you before, and the fastest way to make life work is to make your work work...to make this restaurant work. How you two do your restaurant is how you do your life."

Frank and Jennifer stared at Jonathan.

"Let's begin," said Jonathan. "And I'd like to begin by asking you both a question. And write this question down because we'll be asking it from now on, over and over. Here it is: *What kind of customer do you want?*"

Frank stared at his pad of paper, and then looked up at Jonathan with a puzzled expression. Finally he spoke.

"Anyone," he said. "We don't have enough customers to get choosy. We'll take anyone."

"I know what you're willing to take," said Jonathan, "But I want to know what you want. What's ideal? Who's ideal?"

Jennifer looked concerned. She shrugged her shoulders and said, "Why does it matter when we're struggling the way we are? Why don't we get enough people in here to pay the bills before we start refining the customer profile?"

Jonathan smiled at the business college phrase "customer profile." He said, "I'm glad you're leaving college for a while so we can speak in plain language. This business will get healthy once we start choosing the customers who are most likely to contribute the most to the health of the business."

"We liked *you*," said Frank. "You were the best customer."

"Okay," said Jonathan. "That's a start. Thank you for saying that, because now we're getting somewhere. Why was I such a good customer?"

Jennifer laughed and said, "Because you came in a lot!"

Frank smiled and nodded.

"Once again, in humor we find the truth," said Jonathan. "So write it down. We want customers who come in a lot. We want customers who like to—and can afford to—come back again and again. Those customers will make us strong."

Jennifer snapped her fingers after writing that down. She said, "They're also the customers most likely to refer others, aren't they?"

"That's right. And referrals are going to be how we do our best advertising. Now keep thinking! Who else comes in here often, your ideal people?"

"Bank of America people from down the street, " said Frank. "Some from the GM plant. Royal Oak Little League. St. Luke's Lutheran Church groups."

"Write those down!" said Jonathan. "We're going to build on those. We're not going to build on the radio, and not this way," said Jonathan as he pushed the newspaper with the restaurant ads on it to the center of the table.

"No more advertising?" said Frank.

"No, we'll advertise," said Jonathan. "But not so much and not the same way."

Jennifer turned in her chair to get more comfortable.

"How do we get these customers?" she asked.

Jonathan sat back in his chair and looked at Jennifer and then at Frank.

"I want to tell you both that this is a very fine place to dine," he said. "I like the food, and I like the atmosphere. It feels cozy in here."

"Frank did that," said Jennifer. "He wanted it to be like his mother's big dining room at home. He even used some of her old décor here."

"It's a great dining experience all around," said Jonathan. "And notice that I said the word 'experience.' People need to experience this place. People from right here in Royal Oak. All the best neighborhoods are right here around the restaurant. We'll concentrate on them first."

"Don't we want people to come from all over?" said Frank.

"Sure," said Jonathan. "And they will. But first we must appeal to our best customer base, which is right next door. We'll let word of mouth spread the word out to other places."

Jennifer pulled some brochures from a neat stack of papers she had placed on the corner of the dining table. She said, "These radio stations covered all of Detroit, most of Michigan, parts of Ohio, into Canada, even!"

"That's a lot of wasted money," said Jonathan. "Your neighborhood comes first. If you don't even win over your own neighborhood, you have lost the battle."

Frank said, "We advertise only to the Royal Oak people?"

"We get them in here," said Jonathan. "We give them the experience. That's the key to this whole turnaround. If enough people experience this restaurant, they will repeat the experience and share the experience."

Jennifer looked excited for a moment and then stopped herself. She drew a few vicious circles on her notepad before saying, "Look, Jonathan, how is any of this possible with our cash flow problems?"

Frank jumped up from his chair.

"Cash *flow* problems!" he shouted. "Cash flow problems? Why does everyone say cash *flow*? We have no cash. No cash at all. It isn't whether our cash is flowing or not. There is no cash to flow! We have real money problems. We don't have a problem with flow; we don't have anything to flow. I can make it flow, I just don't have it! It's a money problem. You need money to make money. Everyone says it, everyone knows it."

Jonathan sat back in his chair and allowed Frank to vent. He waited a little while before speaking.

Jonathan said, "Frank, I know that everyone says you need money to make money. I used to believe that myself, in fact. Until I found out it wasn't true."

Frank mumbled something that no one could hear.

"What was that?" said Jonathan.

"Easy for you to say," said Frank out loud. "Sir, I mean no offense, but you, sir, have money. You took care of the Mallis bakery, you have an office in Detroit and I don't know how many music studios. Forgive me, sir but you don't know of this problem. You don't understand this."

"Frank, I do," said Jonathan.

Jennifer turned toward Jonathan and said, "Jonathan, I think this time Daddy is right. I used part of my last business lab time at Wayne State to do research on you. I mean, you seemed to have so many answers; my curiosity got the best of me. You're Jonathan Berkley. You don't just own music studios. You own other businesses, too. You write books. You give lectures at Harvard and Northwestern's School of Business. One major business journal called you 'The Small Business Millionaire.'"

Jonathan looked at Frank's expression of surprise. He turned to look at Jennifer. He took a log while before looking directly at Frank and saying softly, in barely a whisper, "I am a failure, Frank."

Frank said nothing. Jennifer cleared her throat.

Jonathan said, "Not just once, either. I have failed at business four times. And Jennifer, I told you this but you still don't get it. And you, Frank, have not failed once. Not yet, anyway. And I have had four businesses fail. I was broke. In total poverty. I slept on friends' couches because I had nowhere to live. My wife and I were even broke when we got married years ago. We borrowed and bartered for everything for the wedding. I've had it worse than you can imagine, and do you know what I learned from all of it?"

"No," said Frank and Jennifer together.

"It does *not* take money to make money."

"What does it take, then?" said Frank.

"It takes a plan, Frank. A plan that includes people hearing your story. The story of Frank and Jennifer."

Frank and Jennifer squirmed a bit and kept looking at Jonathan. Finally Jennifer spoke and said, "Can you be more specific? Besides what a great cook and person my father is, what does it take to succeed?"

Jonathan said, "First of all it takes a great idea for a product, and believe me, Frank, this place fits the bill. I can eat anywhere I want in the world and I keep choosing here. And then, it takes something else."

"What's that?" said Frank.

"A plan," said Jonathan. "A plan as good as you are."

Chapter 19

Jonathan, Frank and Jennifer refreshed their drinks and pulled their chairs closer to the table.

"What could be our plan?" asked Frank.

"We'll build the plan together," said Jonathan as he pushed an old newspaper page across the table. It was the paper that had the little Sunshine Inn ad in it. The ad looked like a slightly enlarged business card, with some Italian-looking border fringe artwork, the restaurant hours and location, and the slogan, **"Best Food, Best Prices!"**

Jonathan asked, "How much did this ad cost you?"

"Too much," said Frank. "It didn't do anything for us. They said it was because we didn't run it enough. We needed to repeat it more. We ran it five times and then I stopped."

Jennifer said, "It was $200 each time."

"Okay," said Jonathan. "Let's look at why it didn't do anything for you, so we won't ever make this mistake again. And let's start with the concept of repetition."

"It's a good thing," said Frank. "Repetition. No? They all tell me it's what's missing when an ad doesn't work, in newspaper, on radio."

"No, Frank, it's not. Your ad is like a sales person. You send it out into the world to make a sale. If it comes back to you without a sale, it has not done its job for you. Think of advertising like you do salesmanship, and think of your ads as people you've paid to bring in customers."

Jonathan leaned back in his chair and poured some iced tea. Outside the restaurant the lights from the passing cars made flashing patterns on the trees. Jennifer got up to turn up the dining room lights. Jonathan wanted Jennifer and Frank to get rid of this concept of name-repetition, and get rid of it forever. He wanted to think of a way to illustrate the folly in the simplest of terms.

"Okay guys," said Jonathan, as he stood up to pace. "Let's say we have a pie that you don't like."

"That would be pumpkin pie for me," said Frank.

"Okay, let's say I am your server and I serve you pumpkin pie and you don't like it."

"I would tell you to take it away," said Frank.

"Yes, you tell me to take it away, but what if I say to you, 'NO, WAIT! LET ME BRING YOU MORE! TRY SOME MORE! EAT FOUR MORE SLICES AND I KNOW YOU'LL LOVE IT!'"

"You would be crazy," said Frank. "I would be insulted."

Jonathan started walking toward the kitchen.

"Where are you going?" said Jennifer.

"To get more pie!" yelled Jonathan.

"No, stop, I understand!" said Frank, starting to laugh, "We don't have any pumpkin anyway. I made a rule. So I won't smell it in the kitchen."

Jonathan stopped in his tracks, then turned and slowly walked back to the table. He sat down and noticed Jennifer who was frowning and doodling on her pad. She didn't look convinced. She looked up at Jonathan and said, "Give me a better analogy, Jonathan. That one doesn't work for me. The advertising reps always said that you accumulate some mathematical advantage by repetition."

"Okay," said Jonathan, touching the tips of his fingers together and gazing at Jennifer. "Let's do this with math, then." He thought for a moment and looked at Frank and said, "But don't forget the pumpkin pie, Frank, okay? When something isn't good, you don't make it better by repeating it or by increasing it. You don't want more of what's not good."

Jennifer said, "Give me an example that has some math in it."

Jonathan said, "Okay, say you run an ad and it has zero response. Zero. No one—that you know of for sure—comes in off the ad. Follow me so far?"

"I think we can relate to that," said Jennifer.

"Right," said Jonathan. "Zero response. So let's look at that zero. We all know the concept of zero, right?"

"Just look at our checking account," said Frank.

Jonathan smiled at Frank and was pleased to see that Frank smiled, too. Jonathan always believed that the best plans were created when you started to let some humor in.

Jonathan said, "Zero."

Jennifer shrugged her shoulders impatiently and said, "Zero! Okay zero response. We're overly familiar with that! So what?"

Jonathan said, "When you multiply zero by something, any number times zero, what do you get?"

Both Frank and Jennifer stared at Jonathan. Frank held his thumb and forefinger up in a circle to signify zero.

"Right," said Jonathan. "If you multiply zero by five it's still zero. But what if you multiply it by 100? Shouldn't you get a little more for that?"

"No," said Frank. "It's still zero. It's always zero."

Jennifer nodded her head. She got it. She set her pen down and got up to go to the front door where two people were reading the restaurant hours on the door and peering inside to look at the well-lit dining room. Jennifer opened the door and told the couple they would be glad to see them tomorrow if they could come by, but they were closed for tonight. She came back to the table.

"Okay, you got me," she said. "I think we get the picture. Repetition helps the person selling the ads, but not us, not if the ad doesn't work."

"So let's run an ad that really works," said Jonathan. "Let's run an ad that people will read and want to respond to. Respond to like they responded to stories they were told as children. Let's make it huge and fun and irresistible! And if we do that, we can have respectable prices, too. Not 'best prices' because when you have a wonderful dining experience you expect to pay a little more. Like Starbucks. You pay for a great overall experience and quality. You gladly pay. And when you pay more, there's more profit."

"But we can't afford to run a bigger or better ad!" said Frank. "That little ad right there cost $200."

"Well, what if we didn't run it in the newspaper?" said Jonathan. "What if we just printed it up ourselves and handed it out?"

Jennifer perked up. She pulled an accounting ledger out of her pile of papers and said, "We have okay credit at the printer's. It's one of the few places we have paid up...late, but paid up. So they'll want a deposit up front."

"Maybe," said Jonathan. "But maybe they'll play along and help us. Maybe we won't have to pay anything. Anything's possible."

"Why would anyone want to help us?" said Frank.

Jonathan pulled his chair closer to Frank's and leaned in toward him. He said softly, "Everyone's on your side, Frank. Everyone wants you to succeed. Everyone is supporting you. Everything supports you. Even the chair you're sitting on, even the floor the chair is on, even the ground beneath the restaurant, even this good earth, the whole universe is supporting you at every given moment. Otherwise you would fall apart."

"Like I did when I went to the airport," said Frank.

"Yes," said Jonathan. "Exactly. You lost your sense of support. It's back, Frank. Your sense of it is back. It was always there. Support is always there, it's just that people lose their sense of it. It's like not being able to feel your legs!"

"Okay, I feel my legs now," said Frank. "Where do they take me next?"

Jonathan said, "Tomorrow we'll go to the printer's together and we'll let them in on the game of reinventing the Sunshine Inn. Maybe you'll be surprised. Let's all three of us go. When do they open?"

"I'll look it up," said Jennifer.

❋   ❋   ❋

There was a slight misty rain coming down when Frank, Jennifer and Jonathan arrived at Andrew's Printing Company. The shop was at the edge of a small strip mall a few blocks down from the Sunshine Inn, and the owner, Andrew Avery, smiled when he saw Frank and Jennifer come in the front door.

"How's my favorite restaurant folks?" he said as he shook Frank's hand, then Jennifer's and then turned to Jonathan and said, "My name's Andy Avery."

"Jonathan Berkley. Pleased to meet you. We came to talk business with you, Mr. Avery. Do you have a few minutes to sit down with us?"

Andy Avery shrugged his shoulders and said, "Sure, let's go back into the conference room. It's not all that big, but I call it a conference room. Coffee's hot if anyone wants it. Anyone want a soft drink?"

"Water would be nice," said Jennifer, and Frank and Jonathan helped themselves to coffee at the pot in the corner of the conference room.

After he pulled a bottle of water out of the little refrigerator in the corner of the room, Andy Avery said, "How's that young fella you had working for you? Juwan? I heard he got in a little trouble."

Jennifer said, "He's just finished treatment for drugs and alcohol, and I guess he did very well there. His uncle called the other day to bring us up to date."

"Wow," said Andy. "So many young people today get hit by that. I always liked Juwan."

"Good kid," said Frank. "Bad choices."

After they had settled around the table Jonathan began the discussion by smiling at Andy Avery and saying, "I heard you say 'favorite restaurant' when we came in, and I have to say that I agree with you. I don't live in Royal Oak but I come to the restaurant at least once a week because I love the food and just the feeling you get in there."

"Oh, me too," said Andy. "I take the wife and kids after the games on the weekend, and then I'm usually there once a week for lunch, sometimes with a customer to look at layouts, et cetera, right Frank?"

"True, Andy," said Frank. "We appreciate your business!"

Andy said, "I keep telling Melissa...that's my wife...I keep telling her that you are the best kept secret in Michigan! If more people knew about you, we wouldn't be able to get a table there."

"Good point, Mr. Avery," said Jonathan. "That point you just made about being the best kept secret is why we are here today. Frank and Jennifer have asked me to help them.... I'm a consultant of sorts, sometimes...and, anyway, they have allowed me to speak directly with you and share the restaurant's situation."

Frank and Jennifer nodded and looked at Jonathan and back at Andy Avery.

"Mr. Avery," said Jonathan, "you look like you have a very successful printing business here. Can I ask you if it was always that way? If you don't mind telling me. Was it successful from the start?"

Andy Avery almost spit out his coffee and he spluttered to hold back laughter and said, "Oh, my word, no. Oh, goodness, no. We faced extinction a number of times, do you remember, Frank? I used to beg Frank to pay me way ahead of the job. Then I asked you to loan me some money, remember, Frank? Back a few years ago when we were both getting started? And you said you were even worse off than I was?"

Both Avery and Frank were smiling at the memory.

Jonathan said, "Mr. Avery, thank you for saying that, because I want to ask you a question. Was there a point...a turning point, or some defining moment when you knew it would turn around and you would be okay?"

"Yes!" said Andy. "They always told me there would be a turning point, one day when I would wake up and know that everything was going to be okay. I remember the day. I remember the job we got from The Ford Motor Company, Dearborn offices, because Melissa went to church with a woman in charge of getting some brochures made in a hurry. It turned our whole business around and we never looked back."

Jonathan said, "That's something you'll never forget, I'll bet."

"Never," said Andy Avery.

Jennifer said, "We are at that moment at the Sunshine Inn, Andy."

Andy Avery looked at Jennifer and then back at Jonathan, not understanding.

Jonathan said, "Mr. Avery, we are right where you were. We are on the tightrope between total failure and collapse, and final success: being one of Michigan's most beloved and popular restaurants of all time. We want you to be our Ford Motor Company, if you'll hear our plan."

"You want money?" Andy said cautiously.

"No!" said Jonathan. "We want you to accept a trade. We want to print up ten thousand full-page newspaper-type ad inserts, with no payment to you, but a credit in trade at the restaurant so you and your family and customers can eat there for the coming year on the credit you've earned."

Andy Avery said nothing.

"Can we show you our plan?" asked Frank, pulling a large cardboard white board from under the table. "We are going to bring prices up to where they should have been all along, and bring in many, many new lifelong customers at the same time. Can I show you?"

"Sure, Frank," said Andy, pulling his chair closer to the table.

The layout of the full-page newspaper sized ad at first looked cluttered, packed with pictures and headlines and copy.

GRAND OPENING BLOCK PARTY

GODFATHER DAYS at the SUNSHINE INN

AN OFFER YOU CAN'T REFUSE

BRING A FRIEND AND YOUR FRIEND EATS FREE

WE'RE REVEALING DINING'S BEST KEPT SECRET

ONE BIG FEAST ALL WEEKEND LONG

The ad had many customers' testimonials about how great the food was and how Frank was the best cook no one had ever heard of, and photos were everywhere, even photos of DiMaggio and Frank's wife and a photo of Jennifer tossing away books with the small headline: JENNIFER MILLS DROPS OUT OF COLLEGE TO JOIN THE EXCITEMENT! and a photo of the Red Wings hoisting the Stanley Cup with Frank's quotes about how he created Frank's Famous Red Wings.

The ad was a massive collage of excitement and enthusiasm and the joy of cooking. There was even one of Frank's favorite recipes in the lower corner with a MYSTERY INGREDIENT in bold and the invitation to "bring this ad in to meet Frank and learn the mystery ingredient" for his delicious tilapia pasta salad.

The ad also had a special section for FREE DESSERT and COFFEE if "You're with one of These Preferred Customer Groups: Bank of America Main St. Branch, GM Plant 35, Royal Oak, St. Luke's Lutheran Church or the Royal Oak Little League." Those were the four "ideal customers" Frank and Jennifer had identified to Jonathan earlier as people they would like to see more of.

Andy Avery read the ad from top to bottom smiling and shaking his head.

"Well, now you got me excited," Andy Avery said. "I'm bringing the family to this. But there's so much in this ad, it looks like a full editorial page of copy and photos, do you think it will get anyone's attention? I mean, the paper's so full of clutter already; don't you have to be simple to stand out? How will people even find this ad?"

Jonathan pointed to the listed of preferred businesses and groups for free dessert and coffee and said, "Look, this ad will find *them*."

"They will find it," said Frank, "because we are going to hand it to them. They will find it in their hands. It's not going in the paper, Andy, it's being delivered. We've got three of our softball teams trading their time to hand these out all over Royal Oak, every business, every home. In return, they can have their end of season banquets on us. We're asking you, Andy, if you'll trade, too. It's a survival thing for us, and it would be very, very generous of you to do."

Andy Avery looked puzzled and said, "Frank, I don't doubt that you've thought this out, but 10,000? Can you really distribute that many with just three teams of kids?"

Frank said, "Mr. Jonathan showed us how to do this. Each team has about 20 kids, so that's 60 kids divided into 10,000. That's less than 200 flyers per kid."

"Well, that's doable," said Andy. "In two weekends' time? About 85 houses a weekend? I used to hit more houses than that when I was a kid with a shopping news paper route."

"Their parents and families are going to help them, too," said Jennifer. "They're really into it. They want the free banquets."

Andy Avery stood up quickly and picked up the white board ad mock-up and said, "Okay. I'm in! You guys mean a lot to me. I have memories, so many memories, Frank, at the Sunshine Inn, I'm in. Let's do it. Ten thousand copies? Bring me the original photos, the copy, everything."

Frank, Jonathan and Jennifer got up and came around the table to shake Andy's hand.

"Two weeks from Friday evening it begins," said Jennifer. "We're putting it all on the line. We've gone to vendors, suppliers, everyone. We've asked them all to join us in this last spin of the dice."

"I'll pray it works," said Andy.

Chapter 20

The big grand opening was to begin at six o'clock on Friday night and Frank and Jennifer were trying to relax in the living room of Frank's home an hour before the special night was to begin.

They had been up all night preparing food, and had spent all day getting the restaurant decorated with posters Andy Avery had made for the event as a surprise gift to them, showing off his new color presses.

"I am sick," said Frank, as he got up from the couch to refresh his glass of sparkling Pellegrino water while Jennifer finished doing her nails.

"Sick?" said Jennifer.

"Sick with worry!" said Frank. "You know we are finished if this doesn't work. We have spent so much, borrowed so much, asked for so much for this evening…this weekend. What if no one comes?"

"Why would no one come?" said Jennifer.

"Because no one has ever come!"

"Well, that's the whole point!" said Jennifer. "Like Jonathan said, we have never really given anyone a *reason* to come. Now we have. Our handout told our story! We've never really told our whole story—all that we do, what people think of us. Who you really are! We were just getting our name out there. Now we're telling our whole story, recipes, photos, you and me, commitment, customers, everything! There's heart in that ad, Dad. Heart. And information. A compelling reason to come check us out."

"I don't like the feeling I have about it."

"What was our alternative?"

"Close the restaurant."

"Right. And we can still do that, Frank. That's the beauty of going out in a big blaze of glory. You still get to declare bankruptcy if it doesn't work. They'll still let you close. So what have we lost really?"

"I know," said Frank. "But do you know what I worry the most about? Not just that we will lose the restaurant, because I was ready for that already. But that we will lose this thing that has happened."

"What thing?"

"In the past few weeks. This thing you and I and Mr. Jonathan have had together, building the ad, watching the little wind-up toy bump into the kitchen walls and then go out the door, the three of us going to the bookstores. Ralph Mallis's apology! This thing has given us new life and hope. This is the thing I am afraid of losing if this doesn't work for us. If nobody comes this weekend."

"I hear you. I'm glad you're saying what you're saying, too. There has been something different about all of this. Something I can't really describe."

"It is joy," said Frank. "We are feeling, off and on, now here, now gone, but moments…of joy and power. Not since I was a boy do I feel this…."

"Frank, let's go. We don't want to be late to our own…whatever it's going to be."

"Funeral! You almost said funeral!"

Jennifer laughed and put on her jacket as Frank pulled his keys out of his pocket. The drive to the restaurant would get them there a half hour ahead of opening time, and Frank chose to drive there in silence, without his usual Polish music filling the cab of his truck.

As they got closer to the main road to the store, traffic began to get backed up. Soon they were down to five miles an hour, bumper to bumper, with Frank slamming his hand on the steering wheel.

"Oh, no, I can't believe it," he said.

Jennifer said, "We're going against rush hour, not with it, so I wonder what this hold-up is. There's some accident up ahead, I'm willing to bet."

"Another bad sign!"

"Breathe, Frank. Breathe and drive."

"Look at this! I am going to now be late, so if we are lucky enough to have a few customers, Frank Mills is late! What a great message to send! Jennifer, I told you I had a feeling!"

"Stop it with the feelings, Frank."

"I am old country. I feel things."

"Jonathan says to let our emotions process out. To rise above that part of you. Up to where you are when you invent, like when you create a new dish."

"How do you program out how awful it feels to be late to your own...funeral...Jennifer I believe in signs, this is a bad sign, from the Almighty, from wherever...."

Frank's old brown truck finally made its turn onto West Main Street, the road where the restaurant was, usually the emptiest of roads in the evening, and now the congestion was even worse.

"This is really something," said Jennifer.

Soon the line of traffic had stopped completely. Jennifer's worst fears were confirmed when she saw a flashing police light get closer to their truck, approaching along the side of the road.

"Look, it's an accident," said Jennifer. "And I guess it must be a really awful one. I hope it's not one of our people."

"It can't be," said Frank. "They're all at the store."

As the motorcycle cop slowly started to pass their truck on the side, Jennifer rolled her window down and called out to him, "Officer, how bad is it? How long a wait will there be?"

The cop paused, pleased to talk to someone who looked like Jennifer, and said, "It's pretty bad. They've run out of parking up there. So people are going back into the neighborhoods to park and it's backing everything up...."

"Parking?" said Jennifer. "What about the accident?"

"Accident?" said the motorcycle cop. "There's no accident. This is that restaurant thing...some restaurant...The Sunshine Inn...is having some big grand opening tonight, and it's just gotten crazy...."

The cop kick-started his cycle and roared away and Frank looked at Jennifer in disbelief. The traffic slowly began to move again, and as they got closer and closer to the Sunshine Inn they could see the congestion and the lines. There were lines of people waiting to get into the restaurant that stretched for a full city block. As they got closer they could see Vladek and Jonathan putting card tables out in the outdoor mall area and putting table cloths on them as fast as they could move. Jennifer had thought renting those tables and cloths was a bit much, just a little too optimistic, but now they were being put up to accommodate the overflow of people.

"Daddy, I think we have found some customers."

Frank said nothing. He started using the cuff of his white starched shirt to wipe the tears off of his cheeks.

"All my life…." said Frank.

Jennifer was feeling it in her throat, too, but grinning from ear to ear as she looked at her father. She knew how to finish his sentence.

Jennifer said, "All your life you have wanted people to know how good a meal you could prepare for them, but there were never enough people."

"There were never enough people."

❋   ❋   ❋

It was two in the morning when Vladek and Frank turned off the lights in front of the restaurant and Jennifer poured the last coffee for the last table of people in the dining room.

Jonathan and Frank were sitting at a small front table by the window, pouring wine for each other and repeatedly shaking each others' hands and smiling.

"I didn't believe it," said Frank. "And from everywhere. From everywhere they came! How?"

"It was the ad," said Jonathan. "And it was you, Frank. All the good will, all the testimonials in the ad were so *real* that people could tell they were real. When we went around and got those, I knew this would happen. Your story is too good."

"But how?" Frank said. "We only had the flyers delivered here in Royal Oak. Look at those people there. In the corner? They are here from outside of Pontiac."

"Well," said Jonathan. "Let's ask them."

Frank and Jonathan were a little wobbly as they stood to approach the table in the corner. Frank could tell the people at the table were having fun, and he shouldn't interrupt, but he was emboldened enough by the wine to wave his hand to get their attention.

"Good people!" he said. "I want to thank you for coming here tonight, and as you can see we are closing, but take your time and finish your coffee."

"Thank you," said an elderly gentlemen who looked to be the father of the group. "We have really enjoyed our time in your restaurant, and the food was wonderful. Thank you."

"I heard you talking about coming in from Pontiac tonight," said Frank. "May I ask how you found out about us?"

The father figure's wife reached down to pull the Sunshine Inn GRAND OPENING ad-flyer out of her purse, and Frank and Jonathan could see that she had circled the Mystery Ingredient portion of the Tilapia Pasta Salad recipe in the corner of the ad.

"We got a copy of this," she said. "I got it at the clinic where I work."

"A clinic in Royal Oak?" asked Jonathan.

"No," she said. "We're in Pontiac."

Frank and Jonathan looked at each other. No one distributed flyers that far out.

"Everyone in my neighborhood got one, too," she said. "All from the same young man. A fine young man. I think his name was Jermaine."

"Juwan," said the father figure. "His name was Juwan."

The woman put the ad back in her purse and said, "He said he had them printed himself. He owed you a favor or something."

Frank and Jonathan nodded their thanks and returned to their table and sat down. Frank poured Jonathan another glass of wine, but Jonathan pushed it aside.

"No more, Frank," said Jonathan. "I have to drive. And besides, the happiness is strong enough right now, I don't have to add wine...."

"Kind sir, you are a miracle."

"No, Frank, you are. You are the real miracle."

"Why am I all of a sudden a miracle?" said Frank. "We were failing before you. I was no miracle before you."

Jonathan said, "You were, Frank, but miracles are funny things. They don't have much power to change lives until they become stories. They have to circulate. That's all we did here, Frank. We told your story."

Chapter 21

After the big weekend The Sunshine Inn was never again short of customers. Frank and Jennifer had also brought the prices up to where Jonathan had recommended they go, and not one customer complained.

During the grand opening weekend, Jonathan showed them how to have all the customers sign into a guest book and list their mailing addresses and emails to receive special future restaurant invitations and news. From that list Jennifer had compiled an elite VIP membership group. Anyone who had come to the grand opening was now a VIP. Andy Avery's company printed up special full color VIP cards.

VIPs were invited to special free events, like Frank's Choose the Menu Item Night. Members and their guests could sample three new dishes of Frank's and decide which one was the best and should become a permanent part of the Sunshine Inn menu. They could attend that free sample night as long as they brought a friend who had never been to the Inn. The VIP base grew.

Jonathan came in, as always, to enjoy the food and the company, but now he often had to wait in the front area for a table. It was an inconvenience he was delighted to endure.

When the winter came, Jonathan announced that he was going to China for a few weeks on business and wouldn't be around for a while. Jennifer walked him to his car in a light snowfall late one evening and thanked him again for his help.

"It was fun for me, too," said Jonathan. "Keep up the great work, Jennifer, and I'm delighted you're back in school."

"Well, it's part time, because I love this work," she said. "And I'm feeling kind of funny now that you'll be away for a while. Incomplete, a little, maybe."

"What is it?"

"What did you teach us?" she said. "I mean, I know what you taught us. But I'd like to know how you would say it. In a simple way. So I would never forget it."

"I'll email you," said Jonathan. "It's simple. I can email it to you tomorrow before I leave. Is that okay?"

"Sure," she said. "Is it too much trouble?"

"No! It will be good for me."

✻   ✻   ✻

The next day, as Jennifer sat down to get her morning news off the internet, she sipped her coffee and opened an email from Jonathan.

Jennifer:

You asked what happened, and I will now do my best to tell you in the simplest way I can think of.

1. You stepped back from the HOW TO, and strengthened your WANT TO.

2. You stopped trying to GET YOUR NAME OUT THERE and instead, GAVE PEOPLE A REASON to come in.

3. You were willing to stop offering low prices and instead focus on the HIGH VALUE of the dining experience.

4. You and Frank stopped being VICTIMS and became true OWNERS of your business.

5. Finally, you REINVENTED YOURSELVES as a completely successful and customer-passionate business, using the guest book and the membership list to build a loyal clientele.

When you and Frank got absolute clarity on what your intention was—to create a great and prosperous restaurant—you then made your commitment to do so. Most people in business never make that commitment or have that kind of clarity. Instead of clarity they have foggy notions based on hope and fear. Instead of making a commitment, they just wait to see what happens to them. Then they try to deal with it.

When you finally saw how ineffective it was to just "get your name out there" and what a waste of money it was to do that, you were able to give people a reason to come in. You were finally telling your full story, and when people got the story on you, they wanted to come in.

When you brought your prices up, you raised everyone's quality of experience. You raised your own consciousness and standards and you sent a valuable message to your customers that Frank was the best. Your guest book and VIP membership list not only reinvented the Sunshine Inn, but reinvented the restaurant industry, because you know other restaurants aren't doing that. They never even know who walks in and out every night.

And, finally, you stopped being victims. Instead, you took ownership of your success. It was no longer bad luck and ill fortune, it was you. You and Frank really understood deep down that you yourselves were in charge of your failure and success. You took ownership. Real ownership. At that moment, you became unstoppable, and I became unnecessary.

Congratulations. I look forward to my next meal with you.

Be blessed always,

Jonathan

Jennifer hit the "print" function on her computer so she could make a copy for Frank. She wanted him to see what Jonathan had written. As she got up to leave her apartment for the restaurant, she paused at the window to look at the season's first snowfall. It made her remember something, so she went back into her bedroom and grabbed her favorite Josh Groban CD to play on the way to work. There was a fleeting line from a Paul Simon song he sang that she couldn't get out of her head, a line that went "Michigan seems like a dream to me now."

Jennifer smiled as she walked through the snow to her car.

About the Authors

About Sam Beckford

Sam Beckford is the founder of eight small businesses. The first five were massive failures. After business number five he decided to get a "real job" but thankfully got fired after five months and started business number six which made him a millionaire. Sam has shared his business strategies and philosophy with thousands of other small business owners and has personally helped hundreds of business owners across North America increase their personal income by an additional $40,000 per year while working less. Sam lives in Vancouver, Canada, with his wife Valerie, daughter Isabella and son Ben. You can contact Sam Beckford at www.smallbusinesstruth.com.

About Steve Chandler

Steve Chandler is the author of *The Joy of Selling* and a number of other international bestsellers in the personal growth field. He has coached and trained over 30 Fortune 500 companies and hundreds of small businesses. He was a visiting faculty member in the Soul-Centered Leadership program at the University of Santa Monica, and lives in Arizona with his wife Kathy and their pet cat, Grizzly Bear. You can reach Steve at www.smallbusinesstruth.com.

Get coaching from Sam and Steve

Go to www.smallbusinesstruth.com and receive the same transformative coaching that Frank and Jennifer received. Small business owners everywhere are checking out all the goodies available to them on that site to help them enjoy greater prosperity.